OWL MELT WITH YOU

OWL STAR WITCH MYSTERIES BOOK 6

LEANNE LEEDS

Owl Melt with You
Paperback - 978-1-950505-61-6
Hardcover - 978-1-950505-62-3
Published by Badchen Publishing
14125 W State Highway 29
Suite B-203 119
Liberty Hill, TX 78642 USA

Copyright © 2022 by Leanne Leeds

For permissions contact: info@badchenpublishing.com

CONTENTS

OWL MELT WITH YOU

CHAPTER ONE

I sipped my coffee and watched my sister Althea fend off the first customer of the day at our family's new age shop. Athena's Garden was empty except for my two sisters, my aunt, and what I assumed was potentially the female Elon Musk. Despite it being far too early in the morning for ordinary folks, she leaned into the counter with determination.

"Right, I understand, but we—again—don't sell love potions," Althea told the woman in the crisp and professional business suit, tote bag slung over her shoulder.

"Why not?" the woman asked. "Everyone needs a love potion." Her hair was a hard, silvery blond, and she wore it in a high bun. Her frown was stern and businesslike. "This is a magic shop, is it not? You're the Forkbridge witches?" The woman glared at my sisters with a haughty expression as if challenging them to deny the fact. "Why would anyone come here if you didn't sell love potions?"

"Ma'am, again," Althea stared into the woman's eyes, "we're not selling love potions. I can help you with a crystal or amulet that will draw love to you or discuss what goddess statue might help you with your relationship. But we don't, under any circumstances, sell a potion to give a man secretly to make him fall in love with you."

"If you don't sell love potions, then how do you make your living? It doesn't look as if you sell many other things that anyone would want in this place, to be perfectly frank." The woman's voice, high and demanding, had the crispness of a snotty librarian. Her eyes cast around the shop at the books, crystals, candles, cards, and jewelry—among other things—on display, searching fruitlessly for the love potion she was so sure was here. Somewhere.

Ami leaned over to me and whispered, "I swear, I *hate* Valentine's Day."

"Ironic. But I don't blame you," I told her, feeling my mood darken.

I couldn't wait for it to be over. Valentine's Day was the worst day of the year in the human world as far as I was concerned. I'd take a rousing zombie apocalypse over having to deal with this holiday and people like Miss Entitled Stick-up-her-butt any day. Although considering her attitude, I'd guess this woman needed more than a potion to land and keep a man.

"If you're not selling love potions, then you're a bunch of *frauds*." The woman glared at us. "You know how hard it is to find a love potion?"

"Yes," I said.

"We do," Ami added.

"It's near impossible," said Aunt Gwennie.

"Near?" Althea laughed. "It's totally impossible."

"I don't believe you," the woman snapped.

This was getting ridiculous.

"Ma'am, we're telling you there aren't any love potions for sale here," Althea repeated through clenched teeth. "I'm not sure how not selling you something that doesn't exist somehow makes us frauds, but—"

I pushed myself upright and slammed my coffee cup down. "Althea, I think you've put her through enough," I said quietly, moving out from behind the counter. "Your determination has absolutely proven that you deserve—"

"I knew it! You've always had a potion to fix my problems! I knew it!" Her face was awash with joy, and she clapped her hands with glee. "Your love potion!" She pointed at me, barely able to contain herself. "Give it to me!"

"Are you high?" Althea hissed at me.

I ignored my sister and leaned in toward the woman. "Well, now, ma'am, as you can imagine, it's much more complicated than *that*," I said, my eyebrow raised. My sisters Ami and Althea stared at me, confused looks on their faces, but my Aunt Gwennie watched me with amusement. "You see, a love potion can't be sold, ma'am. It has to be *earned*. You follow?"

"Sure," she said, and then she jumped as if I had electrocuted her. "Wait, what do you mean, *earned*?" She looked around, perplexed, as if the question had never occurred to her. Her expression was so surprised and nakedly bewildered that I was convinced the concept of earning something had never so much as tickled her brain.

"Just follow my directions," I said and gestured toward the front door. "Go out the door and get in your car. Whichever direction seems to pull you? Go *that* direction and drive until you reach saltwater—"

"Saltwater?" she asked, surprised.

I nodded. "Saltwater."

"But what if I get pulled north? I could wind up in Canada!"

"Pack a bag?" I shrugged. "Anyway, don't turn right or left, just keep going straight. When you come to a hedge of roses, get out of your car and walk past that. You'll come to a beach. Walk out to the ocean. When you're at the water's edge, jump over the waves three times, but you have to clear the waves."

"Clear the waves?" She sounded incredulous.

"Yes," I said, nodding emphatically.

"Are you serious?"

"As Love Potion Number 9. Once you do that, look down for a shiny black shell with a hole in it the shape of a heart. It'll be hard to find, but it's *on that beach*," I explained with a conspiratorial whisper, looking right and left to make sure I wasn't overheard. "Once you find it, go pick the biggest bloom on the rosebush, and then put both in this glass bottle," I said as I handed her one of the most expensive etched glass bottles we had for sale. "Fill it with saltwater from *that* beach, and then put the bottle on the windowsill for one turn of the moon."

The woman's thumbs were flying over her phone as she took notes.

"After one lunar month—just one—fill a bath with water, dump the contents of the bottle into the bath, strip off your clothes, and soak in it for one hour," I said finally with a nod. "Think about why the man you love doesn't seem to love you back, and Aphrodite will bring you the wisdom to know what you need to do."

"Got it," she said with a nod, slipping her phone in her pocket. "Thank you so much. I promise I won't tell anyone about this." The woman gave me a sharp nod and headed for the door. "You've helped me so much."

"Miss, hold on a moment," Ami said without missing a beat.

"Yes?" the woman said, her nose wrinkling at my youngest sister's Renaissance Faire peasant clothes and wild, unkempt hair.

"That bottle is thirty-five dollars," Ami said, ringing it up. "Will that be cash or credit?"

* * *

AUNT GWEN GAVE me a mock glare, but her watery eyes were twinkling. "That wasn't very nice, Astra, dear," she said. The bell on the door jangled, signaling the entitled woman was off on her possibly futile adventure.

"What?" I shrugged and sipped my coffee. "Better than having some entitled Karen throwing a fit in the middle of the shop. It's too early in the morning for people like her. Actually, I'm not crazy about them in the afternoon or the evening, either."

"I didn't mean that you creating a spell for her wasn't nice, dear. On the contrary, that was very nice, even if you only did it to shove her out without a confrontation. I meant volunteering Aphrodite to deal with that woman," Aunt Gwennie said with a shake of her head. "I don't know that the goddess will be very pleased."

"Think she'll really go out and do it?" my sister Ami asked.

I raised my eyebrow. "Think who will do what? Aphrodite, or the woman?"

"She'll do it, I'm sure. I'm referring to the lady. Actually, I think it was a wise decision to send her on a magical wild goose chase," Althea admitted. "She'll have plenty of time to think while she's looking for that non-existent rock. Maybe she'll hit on the real reason she can't keep a man."

"I could have told her," Ami said and held up *The Tower* tarot card.

I walked over to our crystal table and picked up an obsidian stone with a heart in it. "Not a wild goose chase. It exists. When Archie gets back from menacing the wildlife, I'll have him track her to whatever beach she went to and drop the rock."

"Well, that's service above and beyond," Ami said with a smile. "What if she went to Canada? Or the Keys?"

"She didn't. For some reason, people's intuition always pulls them toward the path of least resistance. My bet is she'll wind up on New Smyrna Beach."

"Look, we sold a bottle at least," Althea countered, crossing her arms. "That was more than I expected."

"I don't get why we even do Valentine's Day. It's so pathetic," Ami said out of nowhere, flopping back into her chair and letting the spiritual magazines fall to the floor in a heap. "We should be celebrating Lupercalia. Yeah, okay, it's not Greek, but it's Roman, at least. I mean, that's closer than Valentine's Day. There is no link at all from Valentine's Day to anything our people celebrate." She flipped her tarot cards over distractedly as she talked and then squinted at the cards in case one of them glowed.

"We don't celebrate Valentine's Day," I told her. "They"—I pointed toward the front door of the shop— "celebrate Valentine's Day, and we sell them every pink, cherubic rock or amulet we can find."

"You mean *we* do," Ami teased. "You run around with the police department."

"We all have our callings," I said simply.

"Forget that," Thea said, waving her hand at Ami as if shooing a fly away from her face. "I love Valentine's Day. Without the church and their St. Valentine, would there even *be* gigantic boxes of chocolate? That alone is reason enough to celebrate and give thanks. I'm telling you. If there was a coven of chocolate witches, I'd join up in a heartbeat."

"If Mom hears you say that, she might turn you into a chocolate witch," Ami said, laughing.

I lit a purple incense stick on the counter, and it burned with a flower-like scent that wafted through the air and mixed with the smell of sage burning in a brazier in another corner. I didn't care about Valentine's Day, the history of the holiday, or anything else my family decided to make some weird significance out of.

I did like chocolate, though.

I mean, who didn't?

"Lavender?" Aunt Gwennie asked.

"Maybe it will calm down the next crazy person demanding a love potion before they get amped up," I told her.

"Good choice. Anyway, Richard Cadbury made the first heart-shaped box of chocolates," Aunt Gwennie called over her shoulder as she straightened statues on a shelf. "In 1861. It had nothing to do with the church. And we don't have Valentine's Day because of some saint. It was thanks to a Chaucer poem written in 1382."

"Is that true?" Ami asked.

Aunt Gwennie glared at her. "Of course it's true. I googled it."

"Sorry."

"I still say chocolate. That's your homework for tonight," Althea said to Ami.

"What?" she asked.

"Google Chaucer's 'The Parlement of Foules,'" Althea said. "Read it and tell me if you think it's a good enough reason for a holiday, or if boxes of nutty, gooey chocolates is a way better one. This should be Cadbury Day. I'm telling you. They should have changed it."

"Honestly, I don't need to," Ami said with a sigh. "I do think the chocolate is a better reason." She looked toward the door leading from the store into our home and sighed. "Speaking of, anyone think Ayla might talk to us again if we get her a big box of chocolates?"

All three of us softly groaned.

My sister, Ayla, was thirteen—no, wait, fourteen years old—and she was every inch that age. She appeared to be a walking, talking bundle of negative emotions with nothing but complaints. She'd locked herself in her room around her birthday in the fall, and even though it was almost spring, it felt like she hadn't come out yet.

Well, not *literally*.

Because we're all witches, some of what I say may sound fantastical, and you may wonder if I mean it literally. But I don't mean she literally locked herself in her room for months on end. (Though, to be honest, I think I'd have preferred that.) She did come out every other day to vent her rage and resentment. So there was that.

"I think this is just a phase," Ami, twenty-one, said as she plucked a card from the tarot deck she'd laid out on the table. "It's just bad this week. Hormones and whatnot." She looked up. "Come on. We all remember what that was like. Puberty sucks."

"I'm not sure she has a 'this week,'" Althea, sixteen, said with some exasperation. "I mean, really, what does her specific complaint matter? What's really new? She's always mad about something."

We all fell quiet, thinking about Ayla and her now-customary mope.

That girl was mad about something, that's for sure. I'd been living with her for almost a year now, and she'd become a real wild card in the family—a title, by the way, I used to wear so often I could have gotten a wild card tattoo. Unlike me, though, she'd thrown a lot of tantrums. Although to be fair, she had been through a lot of changes.

One of which being that I'd come home.

Since then, she'd slowly fallen into some weird funk. We'd all hoped she'd come out of it on her own, but she wouldn't talk to us about it. Ayla felt far away, and she just wouldn't let us in. We tried to speak to her about it countless times, but it only seemed to enrage her.

"You're all beginning to sound fed up with Ayla, and it's not something I want to hear. You're sisters," Aunt Gwen said. "I'd like to remind you that every one of you girls is a little bit different, and no two of you grew up to be quite the same. Your sister Ayla needs your support, not your impatience."

"Aunt Gwennie, I'm not impatient with her," Ami said. "I just don't know what else to do. She's cut us all out of whatever is going on with her."

"She will come out of this," my aunt said. "But what she needs is love and support. Not judgment. Especially not from you three."

As if on cue, the door opened. "Hey," Ayla called out, sticking her head in. "I just went to get my breakfast, and there's nothing left! So did you idiots eat every scrap of bacon in this house, or did the talking bird scarf down my plate?"

"Morning, Ayla! Your plate is in the microwave," Althea called back. "Just take the plastic off before you—"

The door banged shut. Ami, Althea, and I looked at each other, then at the door, then at each other once again. Our eyes met, then finally slid off as if on a slippery slope. Ami sighed.

"This, too, shall pass, girls," Aunt Gwennie assured us. "Just give her time to work through whatever it is she's working through. Just support her until she can hear you. To hear you, Ayla has to stop shouting at the world for just a moment. At that moment, magic can happen. Okay, girls?"

"I guess silence is golden," Ami said with a nod.

"Yeah, well, duct tape is silver," I added. "That'd shut her up for a hot—"

"Astra!"

"Sorry, Aunt Gwennie."

* * *

"So, where's Jason taking you for Valentine's Day?" Detective Emma Sullivan, my best friend and partner, asked later that morning as we drove toward the lavish home of retired teacher Unity Priestpoint for a wellness check. "You're, I assume, finally going to go on a formal date with your boyfriend?"

"One, he's not my boyfriend. 'Boyfriend' sounds like something out of a teen magazine. And I think he's taking me to dinner at the country club," I said, gesturing grandly at the neighborhood as we passed the large homes in Emma's Chevy Malibu. "His mother's a member, and she insisted on giving up her reservations so he could impress me. I'm sure the captain's thrilled."

"You say that like it's sarcasm, but my bet is the captain's super thrilled. He hates the country club, but he knows he can't avoid socializing every now and then while dating the mayor of Cassandra, so he's made his peace with it. I'm curious—are you impressed by a country club?" Emma asked.

"No, but I'm not going to tell Jason that."

"Are you going to finally wear something other than the magical military outfit?" Emma asked as she pulled up to the curb in front of Unity Priestpoint's home. "Because if you do, I have to have pictures. Oh, wait!" She turned the car off and looked at me. "You know the country club has a dress code for dinner, right?"

I stared at her. "No."

"No, you're not wearing that second skin of yours to Valentine's Day dinner, or no, you didn't know there was a dress code at the country club?"

"No, I didn't know about any dress code," I said with a sigh, leaning back in my seat. "Thanks for the warning, Emma. And no, I'm not wearing a dress. You know, this is why I didn't want to go out with anyone. Humans expect all sorts of—"

"Normalcy?" Emma smirked. "Witch or not, Astra, you're still just a woman like any other woman. Besides, I didn't say a dress. I said *dress code*. You don't have to dress like some colonial maiden, but I'm reasonably sure you can't show up for the fancy dinner in a scuba suit."

"It's not a scuba suit."

"You want to explain to them it's super-magic armor that's bulletproof, and that's why you never take it off?" she asked me.

I rolled my eyes. "Let's get this over with, and then we'll talk. Maybe we can go get lunch after this if the old lady doesn't talk our ear off."

The truth was I'd never dated anyone like Jason before. Well, I'd never dated anyone not in the military before. So I wasn't entirely sure what the expectations were for a "girlfriend." Still, I was reasonably sure I had no knowledge of those expectations, passing or otherwise.

We walked up the s-shaped footpath and scanned the windows for movement, but the blinds of the front windows were drawn tight. The house was impressive, a large brick structure with a sprawling lawn and an oversized three-car garage. Emma knocked on the front door.

There was no answer.

"Maybe she's out," I said.

"Maybe she's not," Emma responded. "The daughter has GPS tracking on her mother's car. According to her, it's here." She banged on the door again, this time even louder, her expression slightly concerned. "Do you think she's home?" Emma asked, squinting up at the house. "What I mean is, can you get a sense with your magic fingers?"

"I don't know," I said, slipping my gloves off and touching the front door. My psychometry power slowly bubbled an image of children playing on the street in my mind's eye. I waited and saw a dog run by. Finally, I dropped my hand and put my glove back on. "Nothing. Just a view of the street. Kids. Dogs. Nothing important."

"Darn it." Emma took a deep breath and shouted, "Mrs. Priestpoint?" and banged harder on the door. "This is Detective Emma Sullivan from the Forkbridge Police Department. Your daughter, Liberty, wanted us to check on you. She says she hasn't heard from you in a few days. She's worried. Can you come to the door, please? If not, can you yell if you need help?"

We listened.

Silence.

The house was quiet.

Too quiet.

On a whim, I tried the door, and it was open. I looked at Emma. "Do we go in?"

Emma gave the door a single, measured look

before scanning the front yard and then looking back at the door. Finally, she nodded. "The woman's in her sixties, so she's not that old. But she could have fallen. Had a heart attack. I'm getting a weird feeling, though." Emma reached down and placed her hand on her weapon. "Be careful. It doesn't feel right to me. Something's...hinky."

The official police term for something that doesn't add up is "hinky."

The door opened into darkness.

CHAPTER TWO

Detective Emma Sullivan and I searched the empty house. Only enough light shone through the windows to allow me to see my way around. The hallway lamps were turned on, and the window shutters were closed, leaving the house dark even in the late morning sunlight.

It was an unexpectedly sprawling home.

The ceilings on the first floor were two and three stories high, with chandeliers suspended from the beams. The dim lights reflected off paintings and gilded mirrors on the gallery. The floors were a rich oak, and the walls were a deep brown brocade, covered in artwork. Next to the living room was a small but well-stocked library. Every room I entered, including the bathroom, had a large flat-screen TV mounted on the wall. "No one could afford something like this on a retired teacher's salary," I said to Emma as I stared at the art on the walls.

"She's a widow," Emma responded. "Her husband, Pierre, was a big pharmaceutical dude. He died seven years ago and left her all this—as well as enough to keep her in it for the rest of her life." Emma called out to the woman again, but there was still no answer.

"Then it makes sense that she lives here, I guess," I said as I pointed to a photograph of a smiling woman with silver hair on a large, lavish yacht. "Yacht. She's got a yacht."

"It might not be hers."

"Right." I turned. "Is that the dining room?"

On the left, there was a long dining room table with twelve chairs, a tall silver candlestick in the center, and a china cabinet with more glass doors than I could count quickly. On the right side of the hall, there was a kitchen, a large pantry, and a laundry room with two washer-dryers. A small bathroom at the opposite end of the hall was clearly intended for guests.

"This is a lot for one woman to take care of," Emma observed, frowning. "Why don't you look around in the kitchen? See if there's a note that she was traveling or something. I'm going to go upstairs and check the bedrooms."

I nodded and proceeded to the kitchen. It, like the rest of the house, was deserted. There were no food dishes in the sink or on the counter—nor were there any dirty dishes indicating a recent meal. There were no notes about a spur-of-the-moment trip, either.

Suddenly, Emma called out from upstairs, "I found her!"

I found the detective standing in front of a half-open door in the second floor hallway. "This is a new one for us," Emma told me with a tense grimace. "She's dead. Bullet wound. Don't touch anything, don't get your fingerprints on anything. Just look. No reading the objects. At least not at the moment."

"Got it," I nodded.

The bedroom was reasonably spacious, with a queen-sized bed, bed frame, and headboard carved from dark hardwood. The walls were a dusty rose, and there was a large bookshelf against the wall to the left of the bed. But, on the bookshelf, there were no books. No collectibles, either. It seemed an odd emptiness in a home where pictures covered every available surface.

A trunk sat in the center of the room. It was

crafted from fine mahogany and featured intricate carvings on the sides and feet. More complex carvings adorned the trunk's top, but they were too faint to see in the dim light.

Emma approached it and lifted the lid once more, her hands now encased in nitrile gloves. "Astra, meet the late Unity Priestpoint." She sighed. "Damn."

Unity Priestpoint, dressed in a silk nightgown, was motionless in the trunk and stuffed into it like a rag doll. The woman's skin around her nose and ears was a sickly blue color, but her lips were an oddly festive pink.

There was a single bullet hole between her closed eyes.

"I have to call it in," Emma said, pulling out her phone.

"Wait." I pulled off my elbow-length (psychometry protection) gloves and extended a hand toward Emma. "Give me some of those police gloves. Before the rest of the muggles get here, I want to see if I can read her. It'll be too distracting when everyone else is running around, and they'll all think I'm nuts, anyway."

"What 'everyone else'? They never replaced Jared Upton after you zapped him. And, by the way, did you just compare yourself to Harry

Potter?" Emma reached into her pocket and pulled out another pair of gloves. "You're a lot of things, Arden, but you're no Harry Potter."

"I'm ignoring you."

"What else is new?"

I knelt beside the trunk, my hands on the woman's cold face. I concentrated, closed my eyes, and tried to find the woman's final moments in a sea of lifetime memories. I could hear Emma opening and closing drawers in Unity's room as I concentrated. The dead woman's privacy was no longer relevant.

The images in my mind's eye remained cloudy and hazy, but I could see enough to know the woman had been dead for only a few hours and undisturbed since her death. I told Emma so. "Just what it looks like. No one's touched her since she was shot. She had to be in this trunk when they killed her."

"Okay. That's not creepy at all."

I opened my eyes. "There's something... something important about this trunk." I scanned the wood and carvings, trying to figure out what made this container unique. "I can't see what, but whoever killed her wanted to...hide her in it, I think. There is something about it, though. It seems oddly familiar." I frowned. "But I can't place it."

"Concentrate on her, not the trunk. I have to call the precinct soon, so get what you can. The trunk we can revisit in the evidence room. This might be your last chance with her."

I gently grasped her face again, taking care not to disturb her, and the images resumed.

Unity rolled out of bed. She had been awake, thinking about the upcoming day, when the door to her room was pushed open, and a man entered. So, was it really that early in the morning? Today?

Why did she get out of bed? Was it the man entering or something before that?

I turned to look at him.

He stood tall, had a pale face and dark hair, and was dressed in a black robe that covered him from head to foot. I couldn't see his features. When he saw the silver-haired woman, he grinned wide. Menacingly. He raised a small black gun with a red tip and aimed it at the woman's brow. She collapsed next to the large, unmade bed clutching the tangle of sheets as she fell. The floor next to the bed was stained with a large puddle of blood.

She'd used her last moments to call for help—

"No, that can't be right," I said, opening my eyes. I found myself staring down at the woman's closed eyes. I jerked my hands away and yanked the nitrile gloves off. "I know that she was shot in this trunk. I *know* it, Emma."

"Okay, calm down, Hermione. Wait a minute," said Emma. She felt around in her pocket and pulled out a small notepad and pen. "But?"

"But that's not what I saw." I blinked, trying to make the images come back into focus. "I saw her in her bed, and the killer's shooting her there." I pointed to an area next to her bed. "She fell next to the bed. There. But look, there's no blood. I saw a pool of blood there, and when I look now? Nothing. *And* the bed is made. That doesn't square with what I saw at all."

"Okay. You *feel* the killer put her in this trunk and shot her. Like tickle instinctive feeling?"

I looked back at the trunk. "Yes. I'm sure of it."

"Okay, but why? Anything more than gut?"

I stood up, ran my fingers through my hair, and tried to figure out why I was so sure she was shot in this trunk. Because Emma's question brought up the glaring hole in my claim. I didn't know why I was sure—despite what I saw in the memories of the dead woman—that Unity was shot in the trunk. But I was. The vision of what happened was wrong. "I don't know." I looked at the symbols on the chest again. "Something's hinky." I glanced over at Emma. "Did you find anything else?"

She shook her head. "No, clothes, some jewelry, but nothing that says she was expecting a visitor or that she was shot over there." Emma glanced at the spot I saw in the vision. "Just from a forensic perspective, Astra, I think she had to have been shot in the trunk. Wherever you got that feeling from, I think it's on the nose. I don't know why you're seeing something else with your power."

"Me neither." I looked back at the trunk. There was nothing to hint at the woman's killer, but something about the trunk was...bothering me. Why did it seem familiar? "Okay, let's take pictures of all these symbols. Once we're done here, we'll visit my mom and aunt."

Emma turned and pointed to the symbols carved into the trunk. "You think that trunk could be cursed? Do curses shoot people?"

"Not cursed. But it's certainly...something." I reached out and traced my finger over one of the lines carved into the wood. "I think someone could have used it to...to fake images of the murder, so we're thrown off the scent, maybe. I don't know. I can't feel any major spells on it, but I can't feel anything at all about it. Which is strange in itself." I looked at her. "I need to know what these symbols mean."

* * *

AND I NEEDED to know if Unity Priestpoint was still flying around Forkbridge. Ghosts were chatty, especially right after death. Well, if they stuck around. Unity would know how she died.

Well.

Probably.

I sat in the car as Emma directed what passed for the department's forensic team these days. Jared Upton might have been a jerk, a misogynist, and a secretly evil person, but he had been a useful and experienced forensic investigator. Unfortunately, the guys I saw entering the house were...not.

Ugh, just what we needed. I mean, already, this case didn't make sense.

The top thing nagging at me was the body.

Not to be crude, but the body of the retired schoolteacher didn't smell...offensive. That meant her death had been *very* recent. Internal organs decompose due to cell death twenty-four to seventy-two hours after someone dies. The problem with this timeline? I was sure Emma said Unity's daughter had claimed she hadn't heard from her mother in *days*. When Emma came out to the car, I would check in again and make sure I remembered it correctly, but...

Meh. I did.

I knew I did.

Liberty Priestpoint called the police for a well check because she hadn't heard from her mother in a "few" days. A "couple" would be two. A "few" sounds like three or more. There was no way Unity Priestpoint was dead in that trunk for three days.

Ugh. That trunk.

What was with that trunk?

How had I seen her in her bed and "felt" her in the trunk?

"I don't know how much we're going to get from them," Emma said, sliding into the car next to me. "I could swear I saw one of them holding a book called *Forensics for Dummies*." Emma pulled out her phone and dialed. "Hey, I need a search of all of Unity Priestpoint's credit cards, ATM withdrawals, and phone records." Pause. "Land and cell. Can you pull them together?" Emma nodded at the response. "Thanks," she said and hung up. "They'll get it to us as soon as they can." She glanced at me. "Wow. You look flummoxed. This is really bugging you, huh?"

I gave a nod.

"You think they're trying to hide it from you, specifically?"

I didn't need to inform Emma about the trunk because we'd been working together for some time. She could tell just by looking at me I was growing increasingly convinced that the killer might have used that trunk to conceal the crime details from me or someone like me.

Okay, probably specifically from me.

No one else in the area could do what I could do.

My mind raced as I tried to piece it all together. A spell on the trunk that feigned a murder, but a murderer who still killed. What's the difference? Why is the ten-foot distance from the trunk to the bed such a big deal? It bothered me. "Human crimes are simpler and easier. I don't like that magic is crashing the party."

"Well, this is a human crime," Emma said as she started the car. "It doesn't get any more primally human than murder. Let's go show the pictures to your family."

* * *

EMMA DROVE us the long way home, all the way to the center of town, where my aunt and mother had lived for over four decades.

We pulled into the gravel driveway that led to the colonial-style home. My mother had recently painted it a light lavender color hoping it would provide more calming protection to the fiery occupants within (i.e., my sisters and me). It was also a wise choice because it helped balance out the darker wood colors.

The house was a colossus, with a steeply pitched roof, three gables, and a wraparound porch, that towered over the neighborhood. "Is your mom home?" Emma asked, glancing at the driveway.

I looked around for my mom's car and didn't see it. "I don't know. She should be." I got out of the vehicle. "If not, Aunt Gwennie should be able to help." I walked toward the front door—to find Archie perched on the railing. "Hey, owl."

He looked at me. Then he blinked.

"Archie?"

"Sorry for being late. I got caught up enjoying my last few minutes of not being here," the owl responded arrogantly.

People once believed that seeing an owl was a bad omen or a sign of impending death. Most people now regard owls as pets or mascots solely for their cuteness. That's something I couldn't argue with despite my divine owl's saucy attitude. Archie was absolutely adorable.

"Your loss," I said, smiling. "You missed a murder scene, dude."

The owl said nothing. He just looked at me with his big, wide eyes. The silence went on for a while, and the divine owl's annoyance flowed toward me like waves of cold air off a lake.

My own smile faded. Initially, I'd thought this was just typical sarcastic banter, but something seemed to be…off with Archie. "You upset about something?"

The owl nodded its head. "You couldn't call me? You know I can hear a pin drop in Atlanta! Just say, 'Hey Archie, something is happening,' and I'll come. That's my job. But did you? No." He made a clacking sound. "You know, I don't have the energy to pretend to like you today." Archie waved his right wing and stuck out his head. "I thought we were a team!"

Owls were nocturnal birds, which meant they were awake at night rather than during the day. They could hear well, especially at night—they could hear a mouse rustle in a field or a snake slither over leaves on the forest floor. They could hear a beetle crawling beneath a log.

They could most emphatically not hear a pin drop in Atlanta, Georgia from Forkbridge, Florida.

"You're not going to make me feel bad, Archie," I told him, crossing my arms. "I get that your breakfast excursion to murder and eat small, helpless, cute furry woodland creatures ran longer than you expected, and I get that you're a little sensitive about the divine thrashing we got at Christmas for not working together—"

His cold eyes, shining like black pearls, stared at me from his perch. "You mean that *you* got at Christmas! You play the victim. I'll play the disinterested bystander—"

"Archie!" I cut him off, suddenly annoyed. "We're not going to keep going in circles like this. I don't have the time or the energy. If you're upset about something, open your beak and tell me. If you're just being a butt for the sake of it, give it a rest."

"If it looks like I give a damn, please tell me. I don't want to give the wrong impression." The angry owl's talons scraped against each other as they tapped the wooden railing. "I'll have you know I got attacked! And you don't even care! You're too wrapped up in some stranger already dead to care!"

"Of course I care!" I blinked. "*You* didn't tell me you got attacked; you just started barking at me."

"I did not bark. I am not a dog."

"When did this happen?"

Archie shrugged his feathers. "I was in the middle of a hunt. I was hungry. I was… distracted." The owl looked embarrassed. Mortified, even.

"Archie," I started, stepping toward him. "You and I are a team, and you've helped me through some tough times. It's not a one-way street. We help each other. I want to help you. But I *can't* help you if you don't tell me what's happening. I'm not psychic."

"Your sister is."

I narrowed my eyes. "Why did you get attacked?"

The owl's beak clicked. "It was nothing."

"Archie," I said, placing my hand on the rail.

The owl looked at me. "I can't talk about it here." He glanced at Emma, who was watching the street quietly. "I don't know if she can understand me."

Emma flicked her gaze over to Archie's. "Every word, bud," she said, locking her eyes with his before shooting him a wide grin and giving him the thumbs up.

"I'm starting to think my purpose in life is to serve as a cautionary tale to others. I was attacked!" Archie's feathers ruffled. "I was attacked! It happens, okay!" He clacked his beak and looked down sullenly. "I swear, I didn't think rock bottom had a basement."

"What did I say?" Emma asked me, perplexed.

"Archie, this is pretty dramatic even for you. Come on," I said, holding out my arm for him to hop up. "You can help Emma and me with this case."

Archie sat quietly on the railing staring at me. Finally, he whispered. "I can't."

"Why not?"

He slowly held up a wing smeared red with blood and shook it at me. Then he winced as if in pain. "I can't fly," he muttered weakly.

CHAPTER THREE

I opened the door to the house, clutching the wounded owl. Archie's expression morphed from embarrassed to agonized. His fierce eyes darted around, and he suddenly screeched piteously. "Okay, okay. Mom! Aunt Gwennie!" I called, hurrying into the kitchen. "Archie's hurt! Can you guys take a look at him?"

Emma looked at me, surprised. "You were in the military, and you don't know how to do basic—"

"My mother is one of the most sought-after healers in the world," I told her, cutting her off as I placed him on the counter. "Can I shove a bandage on a wound? Sure. But she's much better at this than I am."

Mom and Aunt Gwennie came charging into the kitchen. Archie lay sprawled on the counter, his feathers ruffled, his head hunkered on his chest. They both stopped short when they saw the owl. "Oh no, what happened?" Mom asked, coming closer. "How on earth did you mangle your wing like that?" She squinted. "Dear goddess, is he still breathing?"

Archie's face went slack, and he slumped to the side. His eyes were half-covered by his heavy lids. His beak gaped open and managed to somehow look pale. All of a sudden, he looked half-dead in the throes of extreme suffering. For a second, he glanced up to make sure he was still being watched and then splayed out again.

Was he kidding me with this?

Emma and I stared at Archie in complete and total disbelief.

"You're such a drama queen. You were just shouting your head off at Astra two minutes ago," Emma said with an eye roll. "You're milking this for all it's worth."

The owl's head poked up, and he peered at Emma fiercely. "Why can you hear me, anyway? This isn't about you. This has nothing to do with you!"

"You squeaked, dude," Emma pointed out. "Everyone could hear you squeak."

"Yeah, but you answered me, so you can hear me talk," he responded with some annoyance. The owl hooted and stared at Emma as if she were his enemy. "You're not supposed to be able to hear me talk unless we're on a star card case, and Unity Priestpoint is most definitely dead, right?" He pointed his wounded wing at her. "No one to save here. So what gives? Ow!" He winced as the jolt of pain shot through his body.

"We can figure that out after we get you patched up." Aunt Gwennie grabbed a towel and started wetting it with warm water. "I'm going to clean his wounds," she said to Mom. Glancing at me, she added, "We have to make sure none of them get infected, and if he flew home—"

"I couldn't fly. So I walked," he said with a sheepish drop of his eyes. "That's why I was so late." In the blink of his big owl eye, Archie went from having the personality of a wounded diva to that of a little kid.

"That must have been difficult for you, little one." Aunt Gwen gently wiped the owl's face, and Archie started purring like he was having a spa day. Done with that, she moved toward the wound and looked closely at his wing. "It's not as bad as it looks. Just a flesh wound, really," Aunt Gwennie said, her face softening with sympathy.

"A flesh wound? It looks like he was run over by a lawnmower," my mother, the uber-healer, said grimly. "Or a car."

"Oh, he does not, Mom," I told her.

Archie sulked. "I am wounded."

"His wing will be sore for a couple of days, and he has a small knot on his forehead, but nothing's broken," Aunt Gwennie said matter-of-factly, dabbing at Archie's wing. "He's missing a few feathers, and the skin is torn a bit, but he should be able to fly without issue once he feels up to it."

"It would be better if Astra carried me everywhere," Archie pronounced.

"Excuse me?" I asked curtly. "I'm not lugging you around Forkbridge. If you're feeling that bad, stay here and sleep it off."

Mom shook her head. "No, I don't see why that would be necessary." She turned toward her sister. "Gwen?"

Archie's eyes bulged as the two consulted. "Make her carry me."

"No way," I said firmly.

"Absolutely not," Aunt Gwennie said. "Now you're just being manipulative."

Archie turned to me with wounded eyes, his little jaw thrust out. "I am wounded and in pain. I'm not asking for much. Can't you just carry me for a little while?"

Aunt Gwennie narrowed her eyes. "Archie," she said, her tone a clear warning.

He drew in a breath and then turned his bright, fierce eyes toward me. "At least carry me up the stairs."

Emma snickered.

Ignoring her, I looked at the owl. "Fine. I'll take you to your roost. But if you're not feeling better by tomorrow, I'm not picking your butt up anymore."

He cocked his head to the side, and a smirk sneaked across his face. "Yeah, fine, that works," he said with a furtive forewing-point, "besides, I got attacked following your stupid boyfriend to that woman's house. Stupid chihuahua ran after me when I went after a stupid frog in their garden."

"Wait, what woman's house?"

"You know," he said, awkwardly preening around his injured wing. "The dead one."

* * *

WE BROKE to get Archie a perch, Ami and her tarot cards from the shop, and so Emma could call the station and get more information from the forensics team and the investigators digging up stuff on Unity Priestpoint. We sat around the living room to hear Archie's story ten minutes later.

"When was this?" Emma asked, all businesslike.

"Just before dawn, so around six? Maybe six-thirty," Archie told Emma, his face serious. "I was hungry, and I heard a frog in the neighbor's back yard. So I went to go get it, and—"

"Why were you there in the first place?" I asked him.

Archie gave a little shrug. "I was following Jason to make sure he wasn't cheating on you. After he canceled your plans for a run this morning, I got suspicious."

He was *what* now?

And what was Jason doing at Unity Priestpoint's house on the day she was murdered?

"What a minute, wait a minute, wait a minute," Emma said, her voice incredulous. "Are you telling me you followed Jason Bishop—Astra's boyfriend—to Unity Priestpoint's house at six this morning?" The owl nodded. "You saw Jason go to her house?" He nodded. "Inside her house?" He nodded again. "You're sure it was today?"

"Yep." Emma looked over at me, and there was a moment of silence as all eyes shifted to follow her gaze. Except for Archie, who added, "It wasn't really a frog, though, you know. It was a monstrously huge toad. I'm not kidding."

"Astra, why did you and Jason not go running this morning?" Emma asked.

The question caught me off guard. "He changed his mind. Said he had something to do."

"And you didn't ask why? Did he have something else planned?" Emma asked, her head tilted as she waited for my answer.

"No, it's not like he's never had to work early before—"

"But did he have to work at six in the morning?" Emma asked, a clear thread of suspicion in her voice.

"I don't know," I said. "I guess it's possible? But, Emma, I have to tell you, I'm starting to feel like this isn't a discussion. It feels like you're interrogating me."

"I'm sorry," Emma said, ducking her head. "It's just...I don't know..." She shook herself and then turned back to the owl. "Okay, go on. Go on with your story."

The owl gave a snort, and his feathers ruffled. "Well, I don't know how that stupid dog knew I was there, but he did—"

Emma gave Archie a wry look. "Jason, Archie. Not the frog."

"Toad." He ruffled his feathers again and looked up at me with his big owl eyes. "He went to that woman's house and rang the doorbell. She came to the door and let him in. I would have gone in to see what they were doing, but I had this stupid yap little dog chasing me. Idiot cornered me in the azaleas."

"Did you see him leave—"

I scowled. "Emma, are you seriously telling me you think Jason shot an old woman?"

Emma looked at me with compassion, and somehow that expression—which bordered on pity—somehow made it worse. "I'm not trying to be suspicious, Astra. I'm just trying to figure out what happened."

"Why don't you ask Jason?" I asked, my voice rising. I could feel the flush spreading up my neck. "I mean, you have a detective's badge, right? Personally, I think you should get to the bottom of this, and instead, you're wasting time interrogating an owl—"

"Astra, a witness is placing Jason at the scene

of the crime," Ami said, looking at me with that same pity-compassion that was making me want to punch Emma in the face.

Emma gave me a sympathetic expression. "Astra, I'm not saying he definitely did it. But I have to look for witnesses and evidence. You know that. Archie is a witness, as inconvenient as it may be. The reality is that Jason was there, and—"

"Look, I know. I get it. I know. Stop handling me like the suspect's girlfriend," I said, interrupting her. "I know. I know what your job is. I know what this means. I just...I can't fathom it. He didn't do it."

"Archie, were you there the whole time Jason was in the house?" Emma said quietly to the owl. He nodded. "Okay. This is really important." Her eyes darted back and forth between Archie and me. "Did you hear a gunshot while Jason was in the house?"

"This is ridiculous," I said, my tone harsher than I'd intended.

"Astra," my mother said with a stern look. "Emma has to do her job."

"I dunno," Archie grumbled, his eyes darting to the side. "The dog finally left, and I hightailed it out of there. There could have been a gunshot.

Could have not been. Who can hear anything over that infernal yapping?"

Emma looked at the owl as if she didn't believe him. "Did you see anything else?"

Archie looked up at me and then turned back to Emma. "No," he said, shaking his head. "Or... wait, no. Wait, wait, wait."

Emma's face was keen, her inquisition expression on. "What?"

Archie cleared his throat, and his feathers ruffled around his tail. "I think I saw Jason leaving the house with a package he didn't come in with. He was carrying something out. He didn't carry it in."

"You're sure?"

The owl glanced at me. "No," Archie said, his face scrunched up. "I mean, it might have been the dog."

Emma frowned. "What do you mean, the dog?"

"Nothing," Archie said, a little too fast. "I was just trying to get out of there. It was a huge freaking dog. I'd never seen anything like it."

"I thought you said it was a chihuahua?"

He froze and then said in a lower, conspiratorial tone. "I'm telling you, I think he was a werewolf. Seriously. Did you see my wing?

No little tiny yappy dog could do that kind of damage."

"It was a flesh wound, Archimedes," Aunt Gwennie said.

"Archie," my mother said, her face stern. "I think it's time for you to go upstairs and rest. Astra?" She turned to me. "Could you bring him up to your room so he can sleep off his trauma? Clearly, it's addled his brain."

I nodded, swooped over to get Archie, and headed toward the stairs. They were getting us out of the room so they could talk behind our backs about Jason. I knew it.

I hated that.

"*Did* you hear a gunshot?" I whispered once we hit the second floor.

"No," he whispered back. "But I don't know what a gunshot sounds like, and I heard a clunk from over in the house. It might have been a gunshot, but it could have been a floorboard settling. Or a door closing. Or an attic fan. Or the dog burping." He looked at me sideways. "You and me, we stick together. I'm not putting your boyfriend in the pokey. No way, not this owl."

"Okay, so what did you see, really?" I asked after we'd reached my door.

He cleared his throat and then said in a rush.

"I saw Jason with a package. I don't know what it was, but it wasn't huge. Left with it, got in his car, and drove away. Like maybe the size of a toaster or a small microwave." Archie nuzzled me before I placed him on his perch. "Astra, look, he didn't look all that upset when he left the house, so either he didn't murder her—"

"Or he's a psychopath," I finished wryly. "Emotionally unaffected by shooting an old woman and stuffing her in a trunk." I sighed. "I know, but still…"

"You're right," Archie said, nodding. "I don't think so either, but that doesn't mean Emma couldn't pin this on him like he's a donkey and she's got the magic tail. And all we got is a feeling. I heard Ted Bundy had a wife, too."

"Okay, harsh," I said, folding my arms over my chest. "So, what do we do now?" I glanced over my shoulder. "What do you want to bet they're all downstairs planning on how to cut me out of the investigation?"

Archie clacked his beak, but he didn't say anything.

* * *

"Astra, we're really going to need you at the shop the next few days," Aunt Gwennie said, her hands clasped in front of her. Emma, Ami, and my mother watched me silently, gauging my reaction. "With Valentine's Day—"

"No. No. I'm not doing it."

"Astra—"

"No."

"What do you mean?" Aunt Gwennie's eyebrows drew together. "We're just asking you for some extra help since your powers aren't that useful for a murder investigation, and Emma will—"

"—learn not to go behind my back to my family if she wants me off a case." I folded my arms over my chest and looked at my mother. "You're going to take her side? Seriously?"

"Astra," she said. "We're not doing that at all. Let's just be adults about this. You know Emma has to investigate the case, and considering Jason is the most obvious suspect, your relationship with him will obviously complicate things for her."

"Are you really not able to speak for yourself here?" I asked Emma angrily.

Emma's eyes widened, and she opened her mouth to speak.

"Okay," my mother interrupted, waving her hands between the two of us. "Astra, you know what has to happen here, and you're not going to make Emma feel guilty for doing what she has to do." She turned to Emma and pointed toward the door. "Emma, I think it's best if you go do what you need to do."

"We can take care of this," Aunt Gwennie said firmly. "Astra, you stay here, and we'll work on the murder together. We'll solve it together."

"I'm sorry, we'll what now?" I asked, shocked. My mother and Aunt Gwennie hadn't been involved in a police case or a star card case, not really.

Emma's eyes narrowed. "Yeah, you'll what now? This wasn't part of the deal."

I shook my head. "A deal? Man, you really never listen to a thing I tell you about these two women, do you?"

"Well, there wasn't a deal, and you two are acting a little childish," Aunt Gwennie said, rubbing her cheek. "But, you know, Astra, we've been sort of involved in the murders before. We might be able to help."

Emma shook her head. "You all need to stay out of this."

"Well, Emma, dear, that won't happen," my

mother responded, pulling herself up to her full height. "Go on, now, and let us do what we need to do."

Emma frowned at my mother and then glanced at me. Her face fell at what she saw, and then she turned on her heel and stormed out of the room. A few seconds later, I heard the front door slam.

"Did you get them, Ami?" Aunt Gwennie asked.

Ami nodded and handed me a sheaf of papers.

"What's this?" I asked.

"Emma asked the department to send everything over here because she assumed she'd be working here," Ami explained, pointing to the papers. "She gave me the PDFs and asked me to print them out for her." Ami smiled. "I made two copies."

My mother and Aunt Gwennie both nodded emphatically, putting a halt to their secretive planning. "You see, Astra," Mom said, a grin on her face. "We're not as useless as you made us out to be back there."

Aunt Gwennie added, "Now go find your boyfriend and bring him back here before your best friend arrests him for murder."

CHAPTER FOUR

I found Jason in his classroom. He was leaning against the door that led to the stairs leading to the recess area. The walls were a cheerful yellow, and the desks were arranged in orderly rows with a lectern at the front of the room. It was quiet for a middle school; students milled around the hallway, dressed in uniforms of blue jeans and band t-shirts, chatting softly with one another. A clock on one wall read 11:27, which meant it was likely lunch here already.

His head was tilted upward, his eyes closed, as he basked in the sunlight streaming in through the glass. Jason's natural highlights shimmered, and his mouth was slightly open as if he was daydreaming a little. A sense of peace surrounded him.

Well.

Time to puncture that pink bubble of happiness.

"Hey," I said loudly from the classroom door. Jason opened his eyes and smiled at me, his face lighting up. I winced, knowing I had come not to bring happiness but the knowledge he was at the center of a whole host of trouble. "Can you get a substitute in here for your afternoon classes? We need to go."

Jason straightened up and glanced at the clock, then his smile fell. "Why? What happened? Is Mom okay? Did something happen in Cassandra?" Of course he'd assume it was his mother, the mayor of the ghost-infested psychic tourist town.

"No! No, she's fine. I know you know Unity Priestpoint and that you saw her this morning," I said, laying the cards—so to speak—on the table as quickly as I could. "I don't know how close you were, and I'm sorry to tell you this, but she was murdered this morning. Shot, and stuffed in a trunk." The deep green of his eyes wavered as they searched mine in disbelief. "It's true. I'm sorry, Jason."

But you need to process this quickly, I thought to myself, *because that isn't the worst.*

His face got that sick, pale look people's faces get when they're shocked by news. His skin paled to the point where it went translucent. For a second, I regretted telling him—maybe I should have let Emma tell Jason about Unity's death. This wasn't exactly the reaction of a murderous psychopath.

"Oh no," he said, his voice thin and shaky. "Who would do such a—how did you find out?"

"We did a well check on her this morning. Me and Emma—and Emma's really why I'm here." He looked confused. "I wish I could sit here and have a conversation about her, how you knew her, and what a nice lady she was, but we need to have that conversation back at my place," I told him, hitching my thumb toward the door. "Archie told Emma he saw you there, and now you're person of interest numero uno."

"Me?" Jason's face clouded with confusion. "Well, yeah, I stopped by to—Astra, I didn't *kill* the woman. Surely Emma doesn't think I would—"

"Look, I know," I said, cutting him off. "But it seems like once Archie made it clear he saw you, she got all paranoid suspicious, and detective-like." I glanced behind me toward the door to make sure Jason and I were still alone. "You have to get out of here. Come back home with me. My family's going to help figure this out."

Jason frowned. "I don't want her to think I had anything to do with this. I don't know how she got that impression, but if she has it, leaving my job in the middle of the day isn't going to make me look more innocent here." He ran his thumbnail nervously up and down the crease of his pants leg as his brain raced through the alien scenario. "Won't she just think I have something to hide?"

"I believe you should stop worrying about making a good impression on Emma the detective and instead focus on finding out who murdered the retired teacher you visited this morning," I told him, feeling like the world's biggest jerk.

Of course he didn't kill Unity. Who on earth would think Jason—sweet, middle-school teacher Jason—was a murderer?

Oh, right.

Emma.

He pressed his fingers to his temples. "Okay. Okay. Let me call the front office. No, wait, I'll just go. There's probably a substitute floating around here, somewhere." Jason glanced toward the window. "Wait. What about my car? Do I leave my car here?" he wondered aloud. "Do I follow you back to your house?"

"Is there any proof that you murdered an elderly woman tucked into the nooks and crannies of your car?"

"What the heck kind of question is that?" He looked at me with innocent helplessness. "No! Of course not!"

"Then leave it," I said. "She'll probably impound and process it, and if Emma's worried about the car and its evidence, she'd be a little too distracted to chase after me." Jason shot me an odd look. "Um, I mean you."

Yeah, okay, I probably did mean me.

Because Emma and I would be at odds at some point.

Directly.

But I really, *really* wanted to avoid that.

Or at least postpone it for as long as possible.

Jason dashed to the administrative office, where he would no doubt struggle to explain his sudden need for the afternoon off.

While he was gone, I looked at the lessons and

educational presentations on the display boards. One heralded the value of math. Another was packed with information about our natural resources in Florida. The largest bulletin board was blank, a gaping emptiness waiting for the next dazzling set of construction-paper facts.

A teacher's aide was floating around the school, and she dashed into the classroom right behind Jason, but he looked so frazzled that it didn't seem as if he noticed her.

"Mr. Bishop?" Had this been a high school, the young woman with long brown hair could have easily been mistaken for a student. She looked that young. Or I was getting that old. "You wanted to see me?"

"Hey, Ms. Girard," he said to the woman. "I'm going to be out unexpectedly for the rest of the day."

"What happened?" she asked, looking concerned. "Is your mom all right?"

The mayor would be gratified to know how many people thought about her welfare.

"Oh, she's fine," he said quickly. "I just, um..." Jason glanced at me and then back to Ms. Girard. "There's something I need to take care of."

"Okay. Any specific instructions or anything else I can do?"

"The lesson plans are in my desk, top drawer. Beyond that, nothing, really. So I think that covers it," Jason said. "I should be back tomorrow. Thank you for covering for me."

I didn't think he would be back tomorrow.

But I didn't say anything.

One day at a time.

Jason turned on his heel and left.

I followed him out of the classroom, through the halls, and down the steps to the door. A few people in the hall gave the two of us a strange look. One family came to a dead stop in the hallway as if I were a contagious disease, and they were trying to avoid getting too close.

"Hi there," Jason nodded, smiling tensely. "How are you?"

They murmured greetings as they watched us pass.

"Rude," I muttered.

"Your outfit's pretty out of place here," he said with a grin. Then, the grin dropped as if he suddenly remembered why I was here and what was going on.

"Yeah, yeah, I know. So everyone keeps telling me," I told him as we slipped out of the side door and headed down the sidewalk toward my car. "Someday, I might care more about what people think than stopping a bullet or a magical attack, but that day ain't today."

* * *

ON THE WAY HOME, I gave Jason a rundown of what happened this morning, how we'd found Unity, and why we were over there. Jason sat silently in the passenger seat of the Jeep. He listened to the complete account from beginning to end without asking any questions or making any comments. But as we pulled up to the house and parked, he looked at me with confusion.

"What?" I asked him, turning off the car. "You have a look."

"You said Unity's daughter called the police for a wellness check on her mother?"

I nodded. "That's what Emma said."

Jason frowned. "That doesn't make any sense," he said, sounding almost puzzled. "Liberty—her daughter—lives in Forkbridge. Just ten minutes from her mother's house, if I remember correctly." He looked at me. "If she was worried about her mother, why wouldn't she just go over to the house and check on her?"

"I don't know," I told him. "Maybe she didn't want to?"

"Why wouldn't she want to?" he asked me. "It's her own mother. If I was worried about my mother, I'd sure as heck head right over to her house and make sure she was okay."

I got out of the car. "That sounds reasonable. Maybe they had a fight, and she didn't want to talk to her mother?" I offered.

"Maybe." Jason didn't sound convinced. Before we went inside, Jason stopped on the porch and looked back at me. "You haven't asked me what I was doing there this morning."

"I have not. In there"—I pointed toward the front door just past him—"there's a gaggle of women trying to figure out what happened this morning. I got you up to speed in the car. Now, you need to get all of us up to speed with what you know regarding this morning and what you saw."

"It was just about—"

I held up my hand. "Stop. Tell everyone. Not just me. I want everyone to hear the same thing at the same time, so no one misses anything, and nothing gets lost in a game of telephone."

He looked pained for some reason, but nodded reluctantly. "Come on. Let's get this over with."

* * *

"Hi," I said, a little too brightly. "We're back."

No one noticed.

Three women surrounded a cauldron—which had been dragged out into the center of the living room—like a scene from Macbeth. My mother, aunt, and sister Ami stared into the bubbling depths as they consulted with one another on…something.

I cleared my throat. "Uh, guys?"

"Astra! It's about time you got back," my mother said with a glance and a nod. She turned to Jason. "Jason, dear, welcome. It's good to see that you're safe and well." She frowned. "For now, in any case."

Jason looked shocked. "What? I was—"

"Don't bother saying anything yet, dear," she said dismissively. Mom turned with a confused, deer-in-the-headlights look. "You need to go talk to your sister."

"Althea?" I asked hopefully, edging toward the shop.

"Ayla." Mom held her hand out toward the cauldron. "I've tried to call Unity here. I failed. The *three* of us have tried to call Unity here, and we're so far unsuccessful. You need to go talk to your sister." My mother gritted her teeth. "Ayla is...refusing to participate."

"In talking to the ghost?"

"Heck, in anything," Ami said. "Ayla told Mom she quit the coven."

My jaw dropped. "She did what?"

"Your sister's misgivings and resentments regarding us have escalated into a full-scale teenage rebellion," Aunt Gwennie said with a sigh. "We're hoping you can talk some sense into her." My aunt cleared her throat daintily. "Since you once quit the family as well."

They would never let me forget that.

"I appreciate the situation, but how's that going to help? Talking to her again, I mean," I said flatly. "We've been talking for months, and she's not—"

"Not talking to us, dear," Mom said. "Yes, I've lived here with her fury as well. But *this* is different. For the most part, when someone was in trouble, she would—even if reluctantly—render aid needed. She's broken her oath here, now, Astra. She's adamantly refusing to take part in the spell." She turned to Jason. "She's refusing to help you. As you might have surmised, we're trying to contact Unity, but Ayla might be the only one that can. And she won't."

"Yes, but—"

"Astra, I don't believe the focus right now should be on your sister. The question of why she's acting this way should be answered, but this is not the time," my mother said. "But if we're going to talk to Unity, we need her."

"Like your mother said, we're hoping you can talk some sense into her." Aunt Gwennie's eyes flashed with a tiny bit of anger—and considering Aunt Gwennie never got angry, it was nuts. This was the Aunt Gwennie equivalent of murderous rage. "If you can't, we will find another way."

* * *

I KNOCKED ON THE DOOR. "AYLA?" I asked, feeling as if I were standing on the precipice of the world at the edge of a cliff. "Can I come in?"

"No."

I frowned. "You don't want to talk to me?"

"No."

"It's important."

"Can't it wait until later?"

"It can't."

A pause. "Fine. Come in."

I opened the door and found Ayla sitting in the middle of the floor in the middle of the room. She wore a pair of sweats and a tank top, her hair was pulled back in a ponytail, and she had that distant look in her eyes that teenage girls did when they were trying to look preoccupied.

Ayla frowned and crossed her arms, but she didn't get up. "Don't try to guilt me or play me. It won't work."

"All I did was come in, Ayla."

She rolled her eyes. "If you don't want to be in here, leave."

The tone in her voice wasn't angry or bitter. It was just...flat.

I bit back a sigh. "Look, we've talked about this before. If you have a problem with the family, and you want to quit, you're more than welcome to go and do whatever makes you happy when you turn eighteen."

"Thanks for your permission," she said, her voice breaking.

"That's not what I meant, and you know it." I bit my tongue, took a deep breath, and let it out. "Ayla, you are the only one that can call ghosts across distances. Mom can't do that. It's a talent only *you* have. And Jason's in trouble. He needs your help." She broke eye contact and looked away. "Ayla, Jason's never done anything but be nice to you. You care about him; I know you do. Don't punish him because you're mad at us."

"You can't make me help him," she said, folding her arms tighter and looking away. "I'm done. Done with all this isolating garbage. I'm just done."

I didn't know what else to say. I didn't know what else I could say.

I couldn't help but think about my own departure from the family. There was a time when I couldn't live with them and a time when I couldn't live without them. But there was a difference. Ayla was a child.

Just barely, though, I reminded myself.

"I'm not talking about this anymore. I'm sorry. I won't. I'm done, Astra. The one time I needed you to listen, you didn't want to hear anything I had to say," she said, her arms still crossed defiantly.

I didn't know what she was talking about, but her words made me feel cold. Was I the cause of this fury? Did I inadvertently set this off? I knew it wasn't just me, but...argh.

I didn't have time for this.

"Ayla, I do want to hear what you have to say," I said. "If it's important to you, I'm always interested. I swear, I am. And I don't want to force you to do anything. But again—you're the only one in the family that has the ability to call Unity. Will you call her?"

"No." Ayla got to her feet and glared at me. "And if you have a problem with that, I don't care."

CHAPTER FIVE

We were all oddly silent, lost in our own thoughts, as we settled into our seats at the table. Finally, Jason looked up and shook his head. "I don't know. I'm sorry. I never meant for this to happen." He dropped his head again.

Jason sat next to my mom, his head down, his hands clasped together. I couldn't take my eyes off him because he looked so small and uncharacteristically vulnerable. I wanted to say something to make him feel better, but I didn't know what to say.

"Hey, you didn't do anything," I tell him with a nod. "This isn't your fault."

Way to go, Astra, I think to myself. *Real profound sentiment there.*

Jason glanced up, smiled, and looked back down.

"So, to start, I'd like to tell everyone we don't know what the trunk is, not yet. We'll continue to research once Astra goes running off wherever she's about to go (since that's how these things usually happen). I think we should begin instead with what Archie saw this morning. Jason," Aunt Gwennie said with a kind look. "How do you know Unity Priestpoint, and why were you at her house so early this morning?"

Jason looked up. His eyes were so sad. "I've known Unity for a few years. To get my Professional Certificate, I had to serve as an Educational Aide for a year. I was assigned to Unity's classroom." He smiled briefly. "I learned so much from her, far more than any book or class taught me. Unity was an incredible teacher. Anyway," he said, his smile fading. "We kept in touch after that."

"What were you doing at her house this morning?" Ami asked, her voice calm and reassuring.

"We're friends," Jason said slowly. Then he winced. "We *were* friends." Unity was more than just a colleague to Jason, that much I could tell. She was someone he admired and respected. Someone he loved, in a way. "She offered to lend me some decorations and information for a section on local history. So I stopped by this morning to pick the stuff up."

"Where's that stuff?" I asked him.

"In the trunk of my car and my classroom," Jason told me.

I groaned. "Didn't I *ask* you if there was anything in your car that would cause a problem? You didn't think to mention that?" Once Emma searched the car, she would find the classroom decorations from Unity's house, and that would give her the physical evidence she needed to prove that Jason Bishop was at the crime scene.

"No, you didn't," he said, looking up at me. "You asked me if there was anything in my car that would be evidence of a murder or my guilt. And there isn't."

Civilians.

"Jason, the only evidence you were at the house was a talking magical owl's statement," I countered, frustrated. "And Emma couldn't use that. She couldn't even tell anyone. The decorations in your trunk? That's evidence." I looked at the ceiling. "The most ironic thing in the world is that this case would be ideal for Ayla's abilities."

"I know, right?" Ami nodded. "She picked a heck of a time to take a hard stance against witchery."

"The ghost talking?" Jason asked. "I understand how that would be useful, but I don't think it's make or break here. We can always go to Cassandra and ask my mother for help."

"We don't need to worry your mother, Jason. I can likely talk to Unity if she shows up," my mother told him. "What I can't do is call her here the way Ayla can, so we just have to hope your friend stops by incorporeally and makes herself known."

"Right. Anyway, what I meant was Ayla can also translocate things, Jason," Ami explained. "We could have probably gotten the box from your trunk without ever going near the car." She shuffled the tarot cards in front of her mindlessly as she spoke.

"Let's not get off track or stuck on things we can't change," Aunt Gwennie said, holding up one hand. "We know why Jason was there this morning. Emma will, soon, too, so let's keep going. But, Jason, you told Astra that you didn't hear or see anything, yes? This morning?"

He swallowed and nodded. "Yes, ma'am. I just rang the doorbell, and Allegra let me in."

My eyes narrowed. "Hold up. Who is this Allegra person?"

"Unity's housekeeper."

I tried not to show any frustration toward my boyfriend by keeping my face even. But, it was like pulling teeth to get information from him. "I see. Does she have a last name?"

He frowned. "Yes, it's...." He trailed off and thought for a second, then reached into his pocket and pulled out his phone. "Let me pull up her contact on my phone and check her full name for you."

"Please do," I said with sugary politeness.

"Down, girl," Ami whispered. "He didn't know it was important."

Jason nodded. "It's Ochoa. Allegra Ochoa."

"So Allegra let you in," Aunt Gwennie said. "Then what?"

"Then I went down the hall and past the dining room to the kitchen. I grabbed the box off the counter where Unity had left it, thanked Allegra, and then I left."

"You didn't do anything else?" I asked. "And you never actually saw Unity?"

Jason shook his head. "No."

My face probably leaked a little bit of doubt. "Jason, I could swear you said you saw her."

"No, *you* said I saw her," he told me emphatically. "I was in a little bit of shock, and I didn't correct you at the time, but no, I never told you I saw Unity this morning."

I thought back to the conversation and went over it in my head. "Okay," I said, realization dawning. "You're right. I assumed, and I said, but you didn't. Got it. That does bring up a question, though. Well, a couple of them."

"And those are?" Aunt Gwennie asked.

"One: Why wasn't Allegra Ochoa at the house this morning when Emma and I arrived to do a well check? And two: why call the police to do a well check at all for a woman with a live-in maid?" I asked the group. "Why not just call the maid?"

"You're right, Astra. We need to find this woman," Mom said. "She could be hurt."

"Or the murderer," Aunt Gwennie added.

"I'll text her," Jason said. He pulled his phone out of his pocket and tapped the screen a few times with his thumbs. "This isn't the first time Unity's lent me supplies, and I have Allegra's contact information just for that."

"Is she a live-in maid, as Astra said?" Aunt Gwennie asked.

Jason shook his head. "No, she's not. Full-time, but she doesn't live there. She lives with her husband on the east side of Forkbridge. I've been there before. I can find the place." He looked at me. "If we think it's a good idea for me to go."

I thought for a minute. "Honestly, keeping you on the move might not be a bad idea. Harder to arrest someone the police can't find, and there aren't any surveillance cameras in this town that belong to the city. It'll take them a while to track us down."

Jason grimaced and nodded.

"What about all these papers?" Ami asked, holding up the stack of information from the police department. "Don't you think we should go over this?"

"You go over it, summarize the salient points, and we'll talk about it when I get back," I said, slapping my hand on the table. "I'm going to take Jason to Allegra's and bang on the woman's door."

"Be careful," my mother said.

* * *

Allegra Ochoa's apartment complex was a little shabby, but it was clean and not totally unpleasant. There were several cars in the parking lot, and a few of the units had well-kept yards, indicating that their owners took pride in their homes.

The ground floor of the building was U-shaped and utilitarian looking, with a single stairway leading from the parking lot to a small porch and an entrance to the building. I decided to park on the street rather than in the lot in front of the building.

"I'll go in," Jason told me, getting out of the car. "You wait here."

"The hell that's going to happen, Bishop," I said, grabbing his arm so hard he winced. "You need to stay in the Jeep." I reached behind the passenger seat, pulled out my ensorcelled protection rock, or MIEPr, and handed it to Jason. "Once I leave the vehicle and close the door, say 'corium.' Oh, make sure you're holding the rock with both hands when you do. Once you do that, no one will notice you."

"What happens if I'm not holding it with both hands?"

"You'll blow up."

He turned white and stared at the rock like it was a venomous snake.

"I'm kidding," I said. "The spell won't work. It needs both hands."

"Don't do that," he told me, his voice breathless from the temporary panic.

"Sorry. Now, remember. Both hands, *corium*. Got it?" Jason nodded as I slid out of the Jeep. "What's the apartment number?"

"Twelve. How do I make everything visible again?"

I walked away without answering.

A few minutes later, I knocked on the door, and it was opened almost immediately by a Hispanic woman in her late thirties. She was wearing a pink sweater and black jeans. "Can I help you?" she asked in a thick accent.

"Are you Allegra Ochoa?" I asked.

"Yes."

"I'm Astra," I said. "I'm a friend of Jason Bishop. I believe you saw him this morning at Unity Priestpoint's?" She nodded. "Oh, by the way, I'm terribly sorry for your loss. I just had a few questions for"—I ran through my brain for a reason to be here—"the insurance. How long did you work for Unity?"

"My loss?" The woman's expression became confused. "What loss?"

I blinked. "Has no one contacted you to let you know about Unity?"

Now it was her turn to blink. "No. What about Unity? Unity Priestpoint is fine."

"I'm sorry, but she's not. She's dead. She died at her home this morning."

"What?!" Allegra shouted, stepping back from the doorway. "Unity's dead? How do you know?" Tears welled up in her eyes. "How could this happen? How could she be dead? I went with her to the doctor just two weeks ago, and he said she was as healthy as a fifty-year-old! Miss Unity cannot be dead!"

"I'm truly sorry, but she is," I said.

Allegra shook her head. "This can't be. She told me she wasn't going to die until she was one hundred, at least!" I followed the woman into her apartment as she sobbed, closing the door behind me. "Miss Unity was a good boss. I can't believe God would take such a kind woman. Dios mio!" We went into the small living room, and Allegra collapsed into a chair across from me. Through the tears, she stared at the floor. "She always said she would take care of me. She would give me a good life, and she would take care of me. Me and

Gabriella. And she has until now. Such a good woman."

"She was shot," I said, "and I'm investigating the murder. Your boss was shot and then stuffed into a rather oddly carved trunk in her bedroom this morning."

"Murder? A *murder?*" Allegra wiped the tears from her eyes. "You're the police?"

"No, I'm not with the police," I explained. "I'm an independent investigator." Well, it wasn't *exactly* a lie. "How long were you and Unity together?" I asked Allegra as she sat back on her couch.

"Together?" she asked, shocked at the suggestion. "Miss, I am married!"

I blinked. "My apologies, that's not what I meant. How long did you work for her?" I rephrased.

"Oh. Oh, yes. I understand. Eighteen years," she said. "I started working for her when I was twenty-four." She looked at me expectantly, but I said nothing, hoping she would continue to talk freely. More often than not, people want to tell you their story, and Allegra was no exception. "My little sister was in her class, and she knew that we didn't have much money after we came to this country." Allegra wiped her eyes with a napkin. "When she got married to Mr. Pierre, she hired me as a maid so I could help my sister go to college."

"That was incredibly nice of her. When was that?"

"I told you, eighteen years ago," she responded almost defensively. "I'd do the cooking, cleaning, and any other chores she wanted to be done. Then, in the early afternoon, she would have me drive her to her doctor's appointments, where I would wait in the lobby. Then I would drive her back home and help her deal with anything she needed." Allegra smiled. "When I was raising my sister, Gabriella, she would let me go to take her to dance classes or to soccer practice, and she would never dock my pay."

I nodded. "When Jason Bishop came over this morning, did he ever go upstairs to visit with Unity?"

"No, it was too early for her to be up yet," Allegra said. "I told him that."

So Allegra insisted Jason didn't go upstairs— but the maid was the one that kept him from going upstairs. "Did you hear anything unusual this morning?" I asked.

"No, nothing. But I wasn't there very long. Just long enough to clean a bit from the night before and get breakfast prepared so it could be reheated."

"Oh?" I raised an eyebrow. "Why not? What time did you leave?"

Allegra thought about it briefly. "It was sometime before eight. I remember that because I was watching the clock. Gaston was supposed to be coming over at eight o'clock to talk to Miss Unity. I wanted to be there to help, but if I'd stayed, I would have been late for my doctor's appointment at eight-thirty," she explained. "The rush hour traffic into Orlando is bad. Very bad. So I had to leave at half-past seven."

"Orlando. That's quite a drive. I don't mean to pry, but are you ill?" Though Forkbridge was a small town, we did have local physicians. So if someone was traveling to Orlando in the early morning, there was a good possibility they had a more severe illness.

"I have the cancer," Allegra said with a brief smile as if it was nothing more than an inconvenience. "In my fallopian tubes." She tapped her midsection the way a pregnant woman would, as if being kind to the cancer would keep it from hurting her.

"I'm so sorry," I told her sincerely.

"Yes, they're sneaky, the cancers. I had it for

many years, maybe, but didn't know. They just found it a few months ago. You see, I am"—she paused, but then nodded and confessed—"here in this country without papers. My sister was able to get the Dreamer papers? But I was too old. So I didn't go to the doctor as much as I should go," she admitted, looking ashamed. "Miss Unity found out, and she was so mad at me."

"For being an undocumented immigrant?" I asked.

"No, no, she was never upset about that," Allegra admitted with a smile. "Miss Unity understood when she found out. She even contacted her lawyer, Wynn Rogers, to try and help me get my documents. But, no, she was mad at me for not going to the doctor." Her eyes teared up again. "She got me in with a specialist and was paying for all of my treatment. I told you." The tears spilled down her face. "Miss Unity was a very good woman."

* * *

I STOOD next to the invisible Jeep and said, "Say '*videtur*,' so I can get back into the car. I'll look like a crazy person if I have to feel my way in." A moment later, the Jeep shimmered into view, and I got in.

"What if someone sees the Jeep disappearing and reappearing?" he asked, handing me the rock.

"They'll go to the doctor and get their eyes checked. People don't believe what they see if they see something they don't believe can happen," I told him, tossing the rock into the back seat. "Well, I saw Allegra. And Emma has not come or called yet. She—Allegra—wasn't even aware Unity was dead. Speaking of, your old mentor sounds like she was a little bit of a saint."

"She was," Jason shrugged. "Did Allegra tell you about her cancer?"

"And that she was undocumented. She and her sister, Gabriella."

"Gabriella," Jason said with a smile. "She is *so* smart. Unity knew she would go to college. She became a doctor, you know," he said proudly even though he had nothing to do with it. "None of that would have happened without Unity's help. Well, and Pierre's money, I guess. But Pierre never would have helped anyone. Unity's not just a saint, but a saint with a heart of gold that has a pocket full of gold," Jason said, shaking his head. "I don't know who could have killed her."

"Did you know that she was paying for Allegra to have cancer treatment?" I asked.

"I had no idea," he said, looking troubled. "She never told me."

"Who is Gaston?" I asked, starting the engine.

"Unity and Pierre's son. He's a real piece of work," Jason said with distaste. "He's twenty-eight, but he acts like a teenage brat. He's always looking for a way to get more money from his mother. Right now, he's living in New York, acting in some stupid off-off-off-off-Broadway play, I think. But, to tell you the truth, I think he's just there to learn how to be a better con artist."

"Wait a sec—Allegra said Pierre and Unity got married eighteen years ago. How is Gaston twenty-eight?"

"It took Pierre a long time to convince her. She thought he was a selfish jerk, and she didn't want to marry him."

"Well, Gaston was supposed to be coming over to talk to Unity at eight," I said, pulling away from the curb. "If that's the case, he's not in New York right now." I glanced at Jason. "You don't seem very fond of him. Just because he's an actor and wants a couple of bucks from his super-rich mother?"

Jason scowled. "It's not just that. He has been

involved in all kinds of shady dealings. Unity told me she had to get a lawyer for him on multiple occasions. He's as wealthy as his father, but he's not nearly as smart." Jason shifted on the car seat. "Honestly, if I were Emma, I'd look at him."

"You really think he could kill his own mother?" I asked, surprised.

"He's lazy, greedy, and he has his hand out for anything he can get," Jason nodded. "Yes. I can see him killing his mother to get his hands on all that money. Or Liberty. She was angry at her mother and at her brother."

"Liberty?" I couldn't parse whether Jason thought Gaston could kill Liberty, or either one of Unity's children could have shot her right between the eyes.

"Unity's daughter. She had her before she married Pierre when she was very young. Liberty always resented Pierre, Gaston, and the money that she never really had," Jason explained. "Liberty was out of the house and on her own by the time Unity met Pierre, and so she watched her half brother get showered with a wealthy upbringing she never had. I can't imagine that was easy."

"You sure know a lot about Unity's life," I said to Jason.

"We talked a lot over the years," Jason said. "As a mentor, she didn't hold herself back or hide her own mistakes. And she mentored more than just my teaching," he admitted. "She was like family." He half-laughed. "Isn't that weird? Unity was incredible to me. Incredible to Allegra, to Gabriella. I'm sure there were more. But to her own kids, nothing she did was ever good enough." Finally, he looked out the window. "Just weird."

"Family is complicated," I told him, my mind wandering to Ayla and the misery that seemed to be drowning her in negativity. I realized it had taken me thirty-four years to give my own mother the benefit of the doubt—and that took the intervention of several Greek gods and a magical owl.

"Yep. Family is complicated," Jason agreed.

We drove in silence the rest of the way back to Arden House, each lost in memories.

CHAPTER SIX

"*O*kay, we need to do a thorough background check on Gaston Priestpoint. I want to know what he was accused of when Pierre's money bought him off with expensive lawyers," I told my mother and aunt as we walked back into Arden House.

Mom turned around and opened her mouth, but before she could say anything, Althea shouted, "Got it!" My younger but more computer-savvy sister had taken Ami's place in the kitchen. I assumed Ami was counseling the shop's lovelorn Valentine's Day miracle seekers. "You have a county and state? It'll go faster."

I looked at Jason and raised my eyebrow.

He thought a second. "New York. Try New

York County first, and then if you don't find anything, spread out to Bronx, Kings, Queens, and Richmond Counties."

"I've got it," Althea said, tapping away.

"I'm impressed you knew the counties in New York," I told him.

Jason hitched a thumb toward his chest. "Teacher," he said proudly. "We're founts of knowledge most people forgot by college."

I smiled. "Good thing. Okay, Thea? I want to know what kind of trouble he was in and who helped him out. And find out when he moved to New York."

"It shouldn't be hard," Althea said. She didn't turn her head when she spoke, and her fingers flew across the keyboard without interruption. "Gaston Priestpoint isn't exactly a common name, even in a place like New York. Well, I would think, anyway."

"All right. Let me know when you get something." I headed back to the living room, which was also partly the dining room, to find Jason sitting at the table in the corner, his face in his hands. His shoulders were shaking slightly, and I felt my heart sink. I was surprised. He was happy just a moment ago—but grief could be like that, I admitted, thinking back to losses in my past. "Jason, we're going to figure this out."

He leaped to his feet and raked his fingers through his black hair, stopping only to gently bite his lip. Jason looked embarrassed at being caught vulnerable. "I know we will. But you heard when Allegra said she left. Unity asked me to come later, to have some coffee, but I was in a rush, so I came early. I left the lesson to the last minute." He breathed out a large sigh. "What if I hadn't procrastinated? If I'd come when she asked me to, maybe I would have been there for her. Maybe I could have stopped this. Maybe she'd still be alive—"

"Jason, you can't think like that," my mother told him, her voice caring and sympathetic. "Every human has their time, their moment when it's time for them to move on. It was simply Unity's time to move on to the great mystery that awaits us all someday."

"Except vampires," Althea called out, still typing.

Jason looked up at my mother, confusion written on his face. "What do you mean, everyone has a time? Isn't Astra's whole deal stopping predestined murders?" I placed my hand on his arm, and he looked at me. "Well, isn't it?"

"Not entirely. I mean, when I get a star card, I'm being asked to stop a death that *shouldn't* happen, not one that's supposed to happen. If it was supposed to happen, it would happen." I think.

"Then you can stop things that are *supposed* to happen. You just said you could. Or Unity wasn't worth saving with your glow card thing." He looked hurt.

"Stop that. That is not remotely what I said. And to tell you the truth, no—we're not supposed to mess with fate, Jason. But what's fate? What's choice? How do we know?" I was getting agitated, knowing that my words held no comfort for Jason. "These powers we have? We can't fully explain their purpose. We do the best we can, and we guess, and even with all this magic power and a batphone in to a goddess, things still happen we don't understand."

"They should pay," Jason said. He clenched his hand into a tight fist. "Whoever did this, they should pay. They should pay dearly." His breath came fast, and his eyes were dark with anger. "I can't just let this go."

"You don't have to, but don't let the darkness eat you, dear," Aunt Gwennie told Jason with a motherly pat on his arm. "We've seen what happens when someone falls into their own black hole. It's not pretty."

"No, it certainly is not," my mother agreed.

"I'm going to try to find out who killed her, Jason. It may not bring her life back, but we will ensure she gets justice. Not vengeance. It's about justice."

"Actually," Archie said sleepily as he shuffled in, his talons scraping the floor, "it could be about vengeance. Valentine's Day is all about vengeance, you know."

"It is not," Aunt Gwennie scoffed.

"It *is*. No one knows whether Valentine's Day originated with Valentinus of Rome or Saint Valentine of Tern. Still, they both have one thing in common."

"What's that?" I asked.

"Emperor Claudius II decapitated both of them," Archie announced dramatically, swinging his wing wide. "Yep. Off with their heads. They bounced all over the dirt road. Vengeful, right?" The owl blinked. "Huh. Makes you wonder why hearts are associated with Valentine's Day and not severed heads." Archie shrugged his small shoulders and tilted his head toward me. "Humans can sanitize almost anything."

Everyone other than Jason looked a little nauseated by Archie's statement.

"You should tell him what I said." Archie pointed to Jason.

"Do you want to know what he said?" I asked him.

Jason looked around at each face and then shook his head. "No, I don't think I do."

* * *

As I sipped my strawberry-watermelon lemonade, I went over everything that had happened in my head since waking up that morning. The strawberry, watermelon, and lemon flavors burst forth in my mouth, and I felt slightly more optimistic about the situation. Thea was so good at the potions—even when it was just a pitcher of lemonade designed to uplift.

Okay, retired teacher murdered and stuffed in an odd, energy-blocking trunk.

I frowned.

That wasn't quite right.

Wealthy widow murdered and stuffed in an odd, energy-blocking trunk. That was probably more accurate, really. I was relatively sure the fact that she was previously a teacher had nothing to do with the bullet lodged in her brain. The money, on the other hand? Piles of crazy money made people do oodles of crazy things.

Okay, suspects.

"Who are they?"

I looked down. Archie had made his way over to the bench against the window and looked up at me from the floor. I used my hand to stroke his feathers, and he tilted his head. "Who is who?"

"The suspects." Archie used his beak and talons to pull himself up, and he settled in an intense ray of sunshine in front of the window. "I can't read your mind, but I can read your face. You're going over what you know so far in your head."

He was shrewd for a bird when he wanted to be. "Yep. You're correct."

"I know. I'm an old bird. I observe. I know things," the owl said confidently, looking at me with his head tilted to the other side. "Well, why don't you tell me what you do know. Like those suspects you were just thinking about?"

"Jason, because he was there this morning and because you ran your mouth in front of Emma—"

"Who shouldn't have been able to understand me," Archie interrupted, his eyes narrowing. "No cards have glowed in the vicinity of this bird, and besides, when it happens, a little bell goes off in my head anyway, so I know. I always know when Ami gets a star card."

I smirked. "Because you get your bell rung?"

"Yes, you ninny, and that didn't *happen* today, so I didn't know that Detective Nosy could hear anything I said." Archie lunged at me to illustrate the point, and I moved my hand away from the owl's sharp beak. He squawked with displeasure. "Spoilsport. I wasn't going to bite." He paused. "Hard."

"Bite me at your peril, bird. Remember, I'm the one that gets you the meat candy from Costco." A few weeks ago, Archie discovered Costco's Extra Thick Steak Strips. He felt it *somewhat* made up for Ami's spell on the backyard rabbits. (To make them taste like ghost peppers so he wouldn't eat them.) "But your point is invalid. When you said it, you *did* know Emma could hear you. And you said it anyway."

"I'm sure you're wrong," Archie said looking miffed. Then he shrugged, looked out the window, and preened his feathers.

"I'm sure I'm not."

"I don't know why we're talking about this. It doesn't matter right now. She's not here." Archie stopped preening and tilted his head again. "Before we go there, let's discuss why we don't put Jason on the suspect list. Are you really sure your boyfriend isn't a sociopath? I mean, he's interested in dating you." The owl's head tilted—as it always did when Archie was particularly insulting. "That's kind of a red flag all on its own if you think about it."

"Jason isn't a sociopath," I said firmly.

"All sociopaths don't murder people. Some just use them," Archie pointed out.

"Are you going to actually offer some help here, or just run your mouth with whatever thought flits through your head to distract me from actually solving this case?"

Archie looked insulted. "I'm helping by making sure you don't dismiss the most logical suspect." I glared. "Okay, fine, you want some help?" Archie pointed his injured wing toward the ceiling. "Have you forgotten that your star power allows you to borrow the witch power of anyone in this house? Your sister Ayla may be sitting in the middle of her room like an emo kid, but if she doesn't volunteer to help, you can just take her power from her."

My jaw dropped. "Archie, that's a horrible thing to suggest. I'm not going to take Ayla's power against her will. My mother can talk to ghosts, and if Unity shows up here—"

"Are you kidding me?" Archie rolled his wide, dark eyes. "If you haven't figured out that your mother's powers aren't anywhere near what your powers are, what your sisters' powers are, then you haven't been paying attention. Mom's a priestess, and she's a healer. None of you can heal as well as she can—"

"She's a high priestess—"

"Yes, exactly! You're making my point for me! Ayla is a death speaker—it's different. Your mother can't do a fifth of what Ayla can do. That's the kid's primary power. You're a—"

"Archimedes, are you interfering in coven business?" Aunt Gwennie asked quietly as she came up behind the owl. Archie looked up and made a tsk-tsk noise. Aunt Gwennie was silent for a moment. Then she clasped her hands together, took a deep breath, and said, "The rest of us can hear you. Minerva is in another room, but she'll be back at any moment." My aunt's eyes narrowed angrily. "I don't care who you are or who sent you here, owl—I will not allow you to insult my sister or say something that will wound her pride."

"Her pride? Her *pride*? She needs to accept that she's not the end-all—"

"Archimedes, she is the chosen one of your goddess," Aunt Gwennie said, her voice vaguely threatening. "You can explain your point to Astra without risking my sister's embarrassment. Considering all she has given up to serve, it's the least respect you owe her."

Archie stared at Aunt Gwennie as if she had grown a second head. Then he huffed, and his feathers flared out. "Fine," he said. "For now."

"Archimedes—"

"Fine! Stop with the lecturing! I get it. But Astra still needs to know, and I'm *still* going to say it." Archie turned toward me. "Some of the problems here have to do with your mother. She's been so focused on holding herself out to be better than everyone that she can't always admit when she's not up to a task. For example, Astra, she cannot see *all* ghosts. Or speak to all ghosts." He leaned forward. "Ayla can."

"I don't understand." I looked at my aunt. "Is this true?"

Aunt Gwennie sighed. "Your mother is a proud woman, and she feels to lead her children, she must be a superior witch to her children. To all that come to her, really." She glanced toward the hallway to make sure my mother wasn't returning. "She's proud of you, Astra, that Athena chose you. She truly is. But your power is vastly different from her own. With Ayla…" Aunt Gwennie trailed off and looked at the owl. "They are similar. Archie isn't wrong. Ayla can see and do far more than Minerva can." She looked up at me. "You may not understand it now, Astra, but Ayla is an extraordinary witch, and she is struggling. Maybe it's time to stop being so hard on her."

"Why haven't you said anything?" I asked, my heart pounding.

"I hoped Ayla could work this through herself. But now…"

"We need her," Archie said with a nod.

"Like, right now? You're sure?"

"Yes, dimwit," Archie said as he turned away from the window. "If you want to muddle through this case by searching for case histories in New York, by all means, keep going the way you're going. But, if you want to talk to the dead, first you need to march up the stairs and figure out what's going on with your sister."

* * *

I DIDN'T KNOCK.

When I walked into her room, Ayla was sitting on her bed, her back to me. A single candle burned on her bedside table, and the smell of lavender filled the air.

I left Archie downstairs. He may have been right—well, relatively—about everything he'd said. Still, I didn't need his acerbic tongue stirring the pot even more.

I shut the door behind me, and Ayla turned around.

She didn't say anything, but she didn't look upset, either. Her long hair was pulled back in a loose braid. She had changed into sleep shorts and a t-shirt. Her thin arms were covered in henna-like tattoos of all different kinds. They hadn't been there earlier.

I'd never seen her look at me with such unreserved, burning hatred. "Ayla?" I asked, suddenly unsure of myself.

"I said what I said before," my sister replied firmly. "And I meant every word of it. I don't know why you're up here, but I don't want you here."

"The part where you won't help Jason, even if he goes to prison for a murder he didn't commit?" I nodded. "Yeah, I heard you."

She looked taken aback at that. "I..." She paused for a moment and then hardened her expression again. "Look, why are you here, Astra?"

"I'm sorry; I didn't mean to upset you by coming up here." I took a tentative step forward, wanting to pull her into a hug.

Honestly, I'm not exactly a hug person. I don't hug. If I've wrapped my arms around you, there's a good possibility you will be flipped in the air and slammed onto the ground.

But I thought the uncharacteristic gesture of affection from me might cross the divide between us—but no. Ayla held up her hand, stopping me. I held up both hands, surrendering to her block. We were still three feet and light-years apart. "Okay. I'm sorry, Ayla. I know we've pissed you off in some way, and I'm trying to figure out how to help, but Archie—"

"Archie?" Ayla's voice hardened. "What does that stupid bird have to do with this?"

Stupid bird?

Ayla loved Archie.

I stared, not sure what I was supposed to say. I didn't have a plan when I came up here. Once I was facing her, I thought I would just—somehow

—know what to say or do to fix this. Or, at least, start to fix it.

But Ayla's face was icy. Her eyes were like a black hole, sucking in emotion and light to create a vacuum that no one could escape, no one could breach.

I was at a loss.

And I was very rarely at a loss.

"What are the tattoos on your arm?" I asked, pointing.

"Something else I can do." Ayla shrugged. "Skin spells. It's not as good as being able to see ghosts or talk to them or sense where they are, but it's useful. They're supposed to ward off evil spirits." I would swear I saw the lines on her arms move as she held them up, bending her arms at the elbow as if blocking a punch.

"They're lovely."

"Whatever." I was still trying to understand what Ayla was talking about when she turned to me, her eyes lit with a fire I didn't think her capable of. "Don't you see? She's just so them. Always. Always, always, always. The most powerful. The greatest. That's all she ever talks about. Any chance she gets, she's telling people what a great witch she is. How she's so much more powerful than everyone else. She's always been a show-off. Even when we were little."

I frowned. "Ayla, I'm not sure I understand what you're talking about. Who's a show-off?"

Ayla glared at me, her black eyes like pools of deepest night. Then she made a noise that sounded…sounded like a snarl. Her eyes glowed with fury…

…then it faded away.

"Sorry, I was just remembering something." Ayla turned away from me and brushed a strand of long hair from her face, shrugging as if nothing had happened. "Anyway, I'm not as good at spells as Mom or even Althea. I don't have the power or the skill. Which is fine, right? Because I don't want to be a witch."

Something was incredibly off about Ayla.

Incredibly off.

"Ayla, it's not about what you want; it's about who you are."

She laughed. A short, sharp, bitter sound. "Who was it that was supposed to be the smart one? Who was supposed to be the one asking all the right questions? Who was it that was supposed to grow up with all this power, only to go and turn into—" She stopped, her face falling. "Never mind."

Was she on drugs? It had to be drugs.

"Ayla, have you taken anything recently?" I asked her. "One of Athena's potions that she forgot to label, maybe?"

"No. I'm not a baby, and I'm not stupid. I wouldn't do that." Ayla's voice had gone flat. Her eyes were empty. She looked down at her tattooed hands and whispered, "I'm just tired."

Just then, there was a knock at the door. "Astra, Ayla? Can I come in?"

"No, you can't!" Ayla snapped back, her voice rising an octave at hearing Jason's voice. She glanced at me with a panicked look in her eyes. "Astra, tell him to go away. He can't come in here!"

Something about her panic tickled a suspicion in me.

She wasn't angry that Jason was at her door.

She was terrified.

"No, come on in, Jason. You're fine." I forced a smile on my face and positioned myself between where Jason would be and where Ayla was.

I still didn't know how much of what Ayla was going through was everyday teenage rebellion and how much of it was...well, something else. Something magical.

But I was leaning toward the latter rather than the former.

In fact, if I leaned any further toward the latter, I'd probably tip over.

Jason opened the door with a smile on his face, walked in, then saw Ayla standing in front of her bed. He froze, his face falling. "Uh, hey, Ayla," he said, stepping back as if worried she might bite.

"Get out, invader," Ayla said flatly. Her face was blank, her eyes hard.

Jason hesitated, then glanced at me. "So, um, I know I'm not a witch and all, but I am a medium's kid, right?" I nodded. "In Cassandra, we all have some skills, like spotting possessions." He pointed at Ayla. "You guys do know that there's a spirit wrapped around Ayla like…like…like she's a dolphin caught in fishing line, right? I mean, you're all witches, so I assume I'm not telling you anything you don't know." He cleared his throat. "But, yeah, she's all tied up by a pretty nasty spirit."

"Who are you calling nasty, you insignificant little worm?" The voice in Ayla's mouth spoke with a deep, gravelly tone that sounded utterly unlike her.

Jason glanced at me out of the corner of his

eye. "I don't think she liked that I called her nasty."

"I picked up on that. Okay, foul spirit that likes to mess with kids," I said, putting my hands up in a placating gesture. "Who the hell are you, and what have you done to my sister?"

And that was how I met my Aunt Gertrude.

CHAPTER SEVEN

*I*t wasn't, of course, immediately apparent that my never-met-her Aunt Gertrude had taken possession of my youngest sister, Ayla.

"Ask your mother who I am," the hitchhiking spirit snarled at me. "Or Miss 'named after legendary Queen Guenevere' who can't think for herself without Minerva's hand squarely up her butt making her talk!" If there had been any part of Ayla in the words coming out of my sister's mouth, it had been purged.

I glanced at Jason. "Get my mother and aunt."

He nodded and went after them.

"Okay, done. Then a different question," I said to the interloping entity. "Why don't you tell me what you're doing here and why you're hiding out in a fourteen-year-old girl?"

"Because I can do it now. Because it was the only way I could communicate with any of you. Because I was resentful at being exiled. Why does it matter? What are you going to do, little girl?" she snapped back at me. "It's not like you have any control here. This was Ayla's decision."

"Do you think I look like a little girl?" I bit back at the hitchhiking spirit but quickly dialed it back. Spirit possession was not something to be taken lightly, and I was unaware of the tangible consequences in the current situation. The spirit's identity was unknown, but Ayla possessed death-speaking and translocation skills and talents. Powers that the passenger might well be able to access and use against any of us or Ayla herself. "Look, we're not going to hurt you," I said, clearing my throat. "All we're trying to figure out is why you're here."

"You can't hurt me. And I'm here to cause trouble, obviously," the hitchhiker said. "Your mother will know exactly why I'm here. It's her own fault, you know."

Knowing my mother, that was probably an interesting story I'd never get to hear. I didn't ask, though. For the moment, I wasn't sure I needed to know. "Look, you're not going to get anywhere by antagonizing me, all right?"

"You're probably right," she said, her voice lower. "But it's fun."

Aunt Gwennie and my mother stormed into Ayla's room. They stopped and squinted as they looked at Ayla. "I don't see any spirits," my mother declared. "Did Ayla tell Jason she was possessed by a demon as an excuse for her recent bad attitude?" Mom gave Ayla a sidelong glance as if dismissing the entire situation. "Honestly, young lady—"

"Now, Minerva, let's stay calm. True, I don't see the spirit, either," Aunt Gwennie said, cutting her off. "But I do recall that Jason said he sensed the spirit, not that Ayla claimed she had one, Minnie."

"She is possessed," I said. "I think, anyway. It's not a hoax, but I can't tell you who it is. I don't recognize the tone or voice of the person talking, but I can tell you I'm almost certain it's not Ayla. Or, well, not *just* Ayla."

Aunt Gwennie and my mother exchanged a brief glance before returning their gaze to my sister. "Ayla, do you know who has possession of you?" my mother inquired, her brow furrowed. "If so, out with it, please."

My sister stared back at her coldly. "It's not a possession. It's a partnership."

Mom's face was flushed with righteous indignation. "I sense nothing. I'm going to assume that this is just your usual teenage drama. And to be honest, I'm not happy with you as it is, young lady. Your sisters have other things they should be dealing with. Important things. So if you have something you need, out with it. Let's plow through this side quest you've devised for attention and get back to the case at hand."

I buried my head in my hands. "Mom," I said, muffled. "This isn't helping."

"Astra, I'm sure I can tell when my own daughter is—"

"Man, she was right about you. Goddess, you are arrogant. Yes, Mom, I know who *possesses* me," my sister said in a completely different tone of voice. It was a quiet, cold tone that was more hers than not, but still not entirely familiar. "It's not a possession, though. It's someone that understands me. Unlike you people."

"Ayla, we're just trying to understand what's going on. Who is it, then?" I asked quietly.

My mother rolled her eyes. "Well, Ayla? What has you acting like this?"

"Mom!" I locked my gaze on her, but she

refused to look at me. Her annoyance and impatience with Ayla was boiling over like a cauldron. "Will you give her a chance to respond?"

"Her name is Gertrude Dora," Ayla said, almost reverently, watching my mother's face with an arrogant expression of smug satisfaction. Mom paled. "Yeah, you recognize that name, don't you."

I frowned. "Well, I don't. Who's Gertrude Dora?"

Ayla smiled an evil little smile. "Mother knows."

I turned and looked at Mom.

Ayla was right.

Indeed, she did.

My mother's mouth was open, and her eyes were wide. She quickly tried to cover her shock with a blank expression, and I wondered what screamed verbal eruption would spew forth from her lips—but Mom remained silent. My sister's mouth twisted into a pleased cheeky grin as Mom stared at her.

"Oh, Minnie, what have you done now?" Aunt Gwennie asked. "I thought you said there was no way to summon her."

That woke Mom up. "I *didn't* summon her.

Why on earth would I summon that wretch? We banished her from our sight after she passed—" Mom looked at Aunt Gwennie. "*You* were the one who said we were good," Mom snapped at her sister.

"I was sixteen! You're going to hold me responsible for a spell I confirmed at sixteen?" Gwennie asked. "Minerva Arden, don't you dare pin this on me."

"What are you two talking about?" I asked.

"Gertie is our sister," my mother said. "Well, was."

"She passed away when we were young. No older than the younger girls are now," Aunt Gwennie explained. The two looked at each other for a moment, then looked back at Ayla. "She was not a very nice person," my aunt added regretfully. "She made our life quite difficult. Especially your mother's."

"She made everyone's life a living hell," Mom corrected. "She was a manipulative witch and got what was coming to her." Aunt Gwen shook her head. "Look, it was a tragic accident, but she wanted to stick around and torment us, to make us live through that horrible night over and over again. I felt bad for her, but it was her own fault. She wanted to haunt the living, and that just wasn't right."

"Don't talk about me as if I'm not right here," Ayla growled in the voice I didn't recognize.

"You're not here!" Mom shouted back. "We banished you—

"From your *sight*. Yes. I heard you." Ayla tilted her head and smirked. "Couldn't see me while I sidled up to your daughter, could you, Minerva?"

* * *

"Whaт?" Althea said once we returned downstairs and explained what had taken place. "Mom and Aunt Gwennie have a sister?" Her eyes grew wide. "And you never mentioned her until today? You two have a sister?" She looked at me, then Mom, then Aunt Gwennie. She squinted at Archie. "Why haven't we heard of this other aunt until today?" Then, in her shock, she repeated, "You two have a sister? Are you kidding me?"

Jason watched us all quietly, Archie perched in his lap like a fat, black cat.

"No, Thea, we don't have another sister," Mom explained with a shrug. "We *had* a sister. Unfortunately, she passed away in a tragic spell-casting accident."

"You mean karma decided to boomerang back

on her threefold fast and whacked her in the head with a dead branch," Aunt Gwennie said with uncharacteristic sourness.

I raised my eyebrow. I had never heard Aunt Gwennie speak with such disdain about anyone. Her judgment about Gertrude surprised me, given the fact that they had been sisters. I mean, my mother could be a pretty bitter pill to take, and Aunt Gwennie raced around defending her like she was a saint.

"Don't look at me like that, Astra." Aunt Gwennie put her hands on her hips. "Gertie decided to curse a boy who didn't return her affections. A witch that would bring a tree down on a boy's head because he didn't like her isn't something that *should* be tolerated in this day and age. Or that day and age. Gertrude's death was probably the fates' mercy, truth be told." Gwennie clucked her tongue and shook her head. "Poor Gertie was a harridan before she was out of her teens."

Althea and I exchanged surprised looks. Our Aunt Gwennie was always the calm one, preaching compassion and understanding. Her harsh assessment of her late sister would not have been out of place in a Witches' Council meeting.

And *they* were overthrown for being authoritarian dictators.

"Harridan? The girl was a psychopath, and I doubt death did anything to soften her," Mom scoffed. "However, your Aunt Gwennie and I concocted a spell that we were confident would solve any haunting issues. We made certain that no Arden woman could see or hear Gertrude's specter and that she could not affect any of us with any dead person magic she possessed." Mom scowled. "That's why her influence on Ayla is so perplexing."

As I burst out laughing, Althea and I exchanged another knowing look. "Are you kidding me? You cast a spell so none of the Arden women could *see* Gertie. *See with eyes. Hear* with ears. Or be affected by magic. Right?"

Mom glared, instantly understanding where I was going with this. "We were young, Astra. We were still learning—and our mother didn't dedicate the kind of time to us that you all had devoted to you for magic lessons. It was years ago."

Mom's dismissal of her apparent mistakes infuriated me.

I furrowed my brow and frowned at her. "It was five minutes ago an aunt I've never heard of told me off using the mouth of my youngest sister, Mom." I wondered if she really couldn't see how her actions may have led to this or if Mom really was that oblivious to the consequences of her own actions. Her eyes flicked to the side and then back to me, as though she wanted me to disappear into the thin air right in front of her. "It was not years ago. It's upstairs on the second floor. Five minutes ago. This is all happening now."

"You know, I hate to jump into this, but you were older than me, sounds like, and *I* would have known to cast a more comprehensive spell than that," Althea said, looking Mom up and down and then turning back to the computer. "Astra's right. You guys made a mistake. One of many in this situation, I'd guess."

My mother stared at the back of her middle daughter's head as if Althea had just broken into a foreign language. "Do you really think now is the time for this, Althea Arden?"

Glancing back and catching the shocked look on Mom's face, Althea shrugged. "What? You're the one that's always telling me to think through all the possible ways around a spell and to lock down the wiggle room. You turned your sister off like a radio. The radio was still there. Other people could hear it. We could all trip over it. And if she caused trouble, none of you would know to stop it." Althea held up her hands. "I could drive a truck through that wiggle room."

"She's right, Mom. Make someone unable to see something or hear something, you know what happens?" Mom looked over at me. "You don't see it coming."

"So, what do we do now?" Aunt Gwennie asked my mother.

"Are you kidding me? Take down your idiotic spell!" I shouted, not caring that other people in the house could hear my anger. "She's talking through Ayla because it's the only way she can talk to the people in this house at all. Remove that limitation, and maybe she'll unwrap herself off my sister!"

"Don't you have something from the Ministry that could do that?" my mother asked. "We just need her out of Ayla, and so I'd have to find the spell, we'd have to figure out how to walk only part of it back—"

I stared at her as if she'd become the child and I was the disapproving parent. "This is your mess, Mother. Yours and Aunt Gwennie's. You need to undo it. Aunt Gertie may be exactly what you say —a mean, ungrateful, ethically-challenged magic user—but if you are right, we need to see and hear her coming."

Right now, however, there appeared to be a slew of candidates vying for that morally dubious position.

* * *

"WHAT A TURN OF EVENTS," Archie murmured as Jason, Althea, and I observed the two older women complain and argue as they rebuilt the elements of the spell they'd used to effectively banish their sister from their lives. "You know, there are phases in a witch's life, and I was warned about the stupid phase. Maybe they're going through the stupid phase."

"When's the stupid phase?" Althea asked him.

"From birth until death," Archie answered matter-of-factly.

"You walked into that," I told Althea.

"I know," she replied, then, overhearing Mom and Aunt Gwennie, she asked, "Why are they talking about manifestations?"

Archie clacked his beak. "A witch's spirit companion manifests itself in several ways. Most often, it manifests as an animal familiar, and it serves as the witch's companion throughout their life. It is a powerful connection and can offer the witch guidance, companionship, and protection."

Althea scratched Archie on the back of the head. "I know all that, Archie. Just because Mom never let us have one doesn't mean I don't know about them. Are you Astra's manifestation?"

"God, no," Archie responded, horrified. "I'm Athena's manifestation. I'm just on loan. And not really a loan. More like a prize." The owl preened proudly.

"You're cute sometimes, you know that?" Althea said, scratching the side of his face. I rolled my eyes.

(In fact, Archie did know that.)

The owl leaned into Althea's hand with a dreamy expression. "Well, sometimes it manifests as a ghost. It can even be the presence of a witch's spirit after death. But a ghost doesn't need to play by the same rules as a living witch." Archie let out a purring sound deep in his throat. "And sometimes, a non-witch ghost can bond to a witch and become the manifestation. Through shared belief, love, bonding. All sorts of reasons."

I blinked. "Are you saying Aunt Gertie is now Ayla's familiar?"

Archie put his head down. "That's about how it reads."

I glanced over at Mom and Gwennie. "They're arguing again."

"They are," Althea said, "and it's really, really, really annoying. I can't believe they can't see the problems they caused with that haphazard spell."

I listened. The two women were sort of jerry-rigging their way through the spell to keep my sister from carrying Gertie without actually allowing Ayla to see or hear her. "They're trying to keep the spell intact." I shook my head. "Mom is so stubborn."

"Yes," Archie confirmed. He turned to face me, raising his head. "What I don't understand is why a witch who was excommunicated by her younger sisters would be so interested in only one of their daughters."

"Maybe Gertie is a better witch than her sisters gave her credit for," I said thoughtfully. "Maybe she saw Ayla isolating and tried to get through to her."

"Or maybe Gertie is just trying to put a stumbling block between Ayla and us," Althea speculated. "Perhaps the whole reason Ayla began isolating was that Gertie whispered deep in her subconscious." She paused. "And maybe Mom and Aunt Gwennie should have told us about this a long time ago."

"Especially given that the wards did nothing to protect Ayla," I agreed. "Hey, speaking of which, how did you miss the hitchhiker in Ayla's head? I thought you knew everything."

"I know a lot, but I can't always see behind people's choices," Archie said, his wing toward my mother and Gwennie. "Gertie didn't want to be seen, Ayla didn't want anyone to know, and those two certainly didn't want anyone to see her. That's a lot of people's hidden agendas to see past."

"So you didn't know Gertie was there until now?" I asked.

"I didn't know," Archie said. "I suspected."

White light erupted from Mom and Aunt Gwennie, nearly blinding me. I held my hand up to my eyes as a figure formed out of the light. I saw the outline of a tall woman in a full-length white gown standing in front of us, her long golden hair braided elegantly over her shoulders. Her face was composed, her eyes deep and sparkling with malice. A pale white halo hovered around her head as if it were an aura.

"Gertrude Arden! You, of all people, are certainly no angel!" my mother snapped. My mother's hand flicked out, and the halo disappeared with an audible pop.

My Aunt Gertie looked at my mother, stunned, and then laughed. In fact, my aunt's ghost laughed so hard that she had to hold on to her stomach and bend over as she laughed even harder.

"What's so funny?" Mom snapped.

"After banishing me from your sight for decades," Aunt Gertie heaved out in between snorts, "the first thing you do is take something from me that you don't think belongs to me. Oh, Minerva, you haven't changed one little bit, have you?" Gertie's body shimmered and wavered as she chuckled.

"Well, that was far more interesting than I expected," Althea said. "Wow, she looks so much like Mom and Aunt Gwennie. Only she's so young." Thea's eyes moved back and forth in fascination. She was still examining the ghost when Ayla burst in.

"It's you!" she breathed. "I can see you! Finally!" Then, with a burst, my sister laughed. A great big belly laugh I hadn't heard since...I don't know, never really. Not from Ayla. Aunt Gertie, her eyes sparkling, joined her in laughter.

"What's so funny?" I asked, totally confused by the events I was seeing.

"Whatever she did to me," Ayla gasped out

between peals of laughter, "it bonded us. I can feel her joy at finally being seen after so many years. She told me I wouldn't be affected by her emotions anymore when she was out of my head because of the spell Mom cast, but she's wrong!"

Mom's expression shifted from rage to utter contempt. "What have you done to my daughter, you dried-up shrew?"

And here we go.

"Mom, dial it back," I told her.

"Minerva, maybe we should all sit down and talk first," Aunt Gwennie said, her face unsure as she watched Ayla and Gertie laugh. "No one was harmed, and we don't know why Gertie's been communicating with Ayla. Surely—"

"Oh, we're going to talk about this," Mom said, perfectly calm and even. "And we're going to talk about it right now." The windows in the living room shook as a gust of wind blew in. Ayla and Gertie's laughter subsided, and they looked at each other before turning to face the windows. Mom ignored it. "Did no one get hurt? Really?" Mom snarled. "Can you imagine how I felt when I discovered my youngest daughter was possessed by the ghost of my sister?"

"Well, Minerva, I will admit I didn't give two seconds of thought to how your sister talking to your daughter through her considerable power would make you feel," Gertie snapped back. "I did nothing but talk to her."

Ayla blinked. "And I was *not* possessed."

"Mom, you really need to stop," I told her. "Archie says they're connected."

"That's not poss—" Mom began, then she suddenly stopped talking. She turned to look at her now-ecstatic youngest child and then back toward Althea and me. "Archie, my sister is not Ayla's manifestation," Mom said. She raised her head and stared angrily at the owl. "It wouldn't be possible."

Archie stared at Mom like she'd turned polka-dotted.

"Did you know sarcasm is the body's natural defense against stupidity?" Archie asked her. With a tilt of his head, he added, "Now, I know this is a tense situation, so I'm trying to be polite, but holding back my razor-sharp wit is making me feel *mighty* defenseless right now in light of your observations." The owl blinked. "I'm just saying."

"Oh, I love sarcasm," Aunt Gertie told Archie. "It's like punching people in the face. But with words."

"I think I like you," Archie said, nodding.

"Can you hear anything that's going on?" I asked Althea and Jason.

Jason shook his head. "I can tell you guys are talking to a ghost somewhere, but no, I can't see or hear her. Her?" he asked me. I nodded. "Her. Or Archie."

"I can see Aunt Gertie. And hear her," Althea said.

"Me, too. But why?" I scratched my head. "I can't see ghosts."

"She's your aunt, right? So you're related to her," Jason told me. "If you're related by blood or bond to a ghost, that connection is stronger, and you're more likely to see or hear them if they want to be seen or heard." Everyone looked at Jason. "Son of a powerful medium?" He smiled and shrugged. "We pick up things being raised in Cassandra."

Ami dashed in, exclaiming, "I just need to get a drink; they've all sold so I couldn't just get one out of the cooler! Maybe someone should do a quick Costco run?" She screeched to a halt as she raced across the room toward the kitchen, staring at the shimmering apparition of our Aunt Gertie. "Um. Hi."

"Hello," Aunt Gertie said with a bow.

Ami looked around the room. "Did I miss something?"

CHAPTER EIGHT

*J*ason offered to work the cash register at the shop so we could figure out what was going on as a family.

And what a family we were at the moment.

We'd quickly caught Ami up on the family drama she'd been blissfully unaware of until her thirst drew her into the middle of it all. We all took turns adding details and attempting to explain. Still, my mother's, Aunt Gwennie's, and Aunt Gertie's disagreements quickly devolved into a shouting match.

Ami stared at everyone as Mom gesticulated wildly toward my Aunt Gertie. "How dare you claim that you were not putting a curse on that boy! I know you were; I saw the rose petals in your room! I saw them! Between that and the cardamom, what else could you possibly have been doing?"

As the tension grew, my sisters and I moved away from the squabbling women. Archie quickly followed.

"I feel like I've just been thrown into the upside down." Ami turned to face Ayla as the three older women argued, their voices raised in frustration. "Why didn't you just tell us what was going on, Ayla?" She was speaking in a low, placating voice. "I truly don't understand why you didn't just tell one of us what was going on. Is this why you've been so angry?"

My youngest sister took a deep breath, her eyes narrowing. "Are you actually trying to claim you didn't know? None of you? With all your powers and all your abilities and all your know-it-all stuff, you didn't know about Aunt Gertie?" Ayla turned to me specifically, fury in her eyes. "Even *you*? No one mentioned her in Impy?"

I shifted uncomfortably, hating that I didn't know what to say. I knew what Ayla was implying, and she was right. We should have known. We should have been able to sense Aunt Gertie. Someone should have told is about her. My mother, Aunt Gwennie, someone. If I were in

Ayla's shoes, I'm not sure I'd believe that none of us knew about it, either.

But we didn't.

"I didn't," I told her. "No one ever mentioned Gertrude Dora to me that I can recall. No one even hinted at her existence. To be honest, I don't blame you for being a bit angry at us the past few months. If I thought you guys were keeping a secret of this magnitude from me, I'd probably feel the same way."

Ayla locked her gaze on me for a few seconds longer before taking a deep breath. Finally, she seemed to calm down. "Yeah, well, considering what Mom pulled with Aunt Gertie, it wouldn't surprise me that you guys were just as much in the dark as I was. So, I'm going to stop biting your heads off and being mad at you. But just you." She shot Mom a look. "*That* woman's out of control."

"Ayla, we don't really know the story—" Althea said, but Ayla cut her off.

"Stop. You always make excuses for her. I know the story. I've been talking to Aunt Gertie for months now."

"You know one side of the story," I said with a shake of my head. "I know you don't trust Mom"—and between you, me, and the wall, I didn't much trust her on this subject, either—"but we have to give her a chance to explain."

"Yes," Ayla said, looking at me like I was stupid. "Let's give the high priestess yet another opportunity to lie to all of us for our own good. We should do that."

"Ayla," Althea said, putting a hand on her shoulder. "I know you've had your issues with Mom, and I get why that is—I mean, let's face it. We've all had issues at one time or another." Thea looked at Ami. "Well, except for Ami, since she's perfect."

"Dude, not cool," Ami told her. "I don't want us to turn into what's going on over there. Not now, not ever. All right?"

"I didn't say it was your fault," Thea said with a shrug. "I just mean that being angry about this isn't going to get any of us anywhere. What's more, Jason's still in trouble, and while we argue about this, we're not getting anything done about that. So just take a breather, and calm down."

Ayla turned on her. "Why don't you get off my back, too, Althea? I'm not the one who's out of control."

Althea looked like she wanted to say something in retort, but I headed her off.

"Ayla," I said, the sincerity in my voice

surprising even me. "I know we don't always agree about what's right or wrong here. I know we don't always agree about what to do, but Althea's right about one thing. Ami, too." I looked around. "We're sisters. Let's not make their problems our problems."

Ayla looked at me for a long moment, her eyes narrowed. "Fine," she finally said—though the look she shot Mom after made it clear that as quickly as Ayla believed and forgave us, she wouldn't be so quick to forgive Mom.

"Good."

Ayla sighed. "Okay, so what do we do next?"

I cast a glance over at the baby boomer brawl. "I think we should give them a minute to sort things out." I leaned back against the counter. "We still need to try and call Unity Priestpoint here, if you're willing." I looked at Ayla. "*Are* you willing?"

Ayla nodded and held out a fist.

We stared, confused.

"What're you doing?" Ami asked.

A few seconds later, Ayla turned over her hand and opened her fist. A butterfly appeared, sitting gently in the center of her outstretched hand. "Okay, go, then," she said quietly. It launched up and fluttered about in the room.

Althea's jaw dropped. "What the—"

"What is that?" Ami asked, her eyes wide as they followed the butterfly.

Ayla just smiled. "Watch." It hovered for a moment, then shot out of the room through an open window into the sunlight. "It will find her and let her know we want to talk to her. Whether she comes here or not, that'll be her own choice."

"How did you learn that? *Where* did you learn that?" Althea asked.

"Aunt Gertie," Ayla said with a shrug. "I don't know where she learned it, though. She told me that since she's been dead, she's learned a lot about magic that the living don't really tend to stumble on much. So she's been teaching me." Ayla shrugged again. "Aunt Gertie says the afterlife is a lot like the mortal world," she continued, her voice confident. "There are all kinds of magic and all kinds of paths to learn magic. Some take, like, years of study to learn, but some only take a moment."

I glanced over at Mom, Aunt Gwennie, and Aunt Gertie. Though the arguing women were still talking in animatedly low tones, their voices were at least calmer. "Maybe they're finally getting somewhere," I said, my voice hopeful.

"Right. It only took decades," Althea snorted.

"And a possession," Ami joked.

* * *

THOUGH IT'S one of the most popular myths in the magical world and one of the most fundamental myths for witches, the idea that witches learn magic from books is, to put it bluntly, a farce. Instead, the majority of magic is taught by another witch, usually in a formal apprenticeship or academy or—if you're lucky—family setting.

From the time I was old enough to crawl, my mother and aunt began teaching me the ways of the witches. It was tradition passed down through generations in our family—in most families, really. We were taught, and guided, and expected to exhibit the same wisdom and knowledge, regardless of the individual nuances of our own powers.

I had additional training at the Ministry, obviously—and I realized as I watched Ayla do something extraordinary that I hadn't been particularly responsible in bringing that knowledge back to my sisters.

Ami's shout brought me out of my deep thoughts.

"Astra!" Ami pointed toward the front window of the house behind me. "Emma's here, and she's got two officers with her. They're frog-marching Jason into a police car!"

I was sure I'd never moved so fast in my life.

My sisters were right behind me, racing toward the front door. Emma and the two officers were standing next to the car, and Jason's head could be seen in the back seat.

"What are you doing?" I asked angrily as I reached them. "You can't take him like that. You have no evidence that he did anything to that woman."

"We're arresting him—well, holding him— because he's a material witness," said one officer. He looked back and forth between us in confusion. "Didn't Emma call you?"

I glared at Emma. "No, Emma didn't call me."

"We're taking him into custody because we couldn't get ahold of him, because he left work, and because he dates someone that used to be—or so I recall—a member of the military that might be acquainted with ways to hide from law enforcement," Emma replied. She turned the page on her notepad and marked something down. "You told me to go ask Jason, and then you went to his school and told him to run." She looked up, her head tilted. "Not for nothing, but did you give even a moment's thought to how that was going to look?"

"No, because he's not guilty," I said, frustrated. "Look, I know you're just doing your job, but you're doing it wrong." I could hear the police radio chatter through the open window. "And I did not tell him to run!" I yelled. "No one's running. Obviously."

"You didn't?" she asked. "Well, whatever you advised him, it looks like you sent him out of the frying pan and into the fire."

Everyone fell silent. All I heard was the police radio crackling through the open window and the rushing of blood in my ears.

I couldn't believe Emma had done this, and without so much as a conversation between us first. "At the very least, Emma, let me talk to Jason before they take him away."

"Astra, you're on thin ice," Emma told me, her eyes annoyed. "I get what you're going through, I really do, but you work at the police department. This is a regular, plain old murder, and we have procedures we have to follow." Emma frowned. "Again, what you did made his situation worse. Remember our deal? Your type of case, your rules. My type of case? My rules. Which are *the* rules."

"You know, I remember a time when your brother—"

"Astra, just let them go. He's at least safe in jail. Well, relatively." Ami put an arm on my shoulder. "We've got this, Astra. I promise. Emma's just doing her job. It's not personal."

Not personal, my a—

"Astra, look at me," Ayla said, her tone pleading.

Grinding my teeth together to bite back my words, I held my tongue and my temper in check as best I could manage. It was difficult under the circumstances, but I didn't want to get Jason in any deeper trouble than he was already in. So, instead, I turned to look.

My entire family, including Aunt Gertie, stood beside me on the front lawn. The customers from the magic shop had come out onto the porch to watch.

Ayla reached out toward me. "Astra, she's just doing her job. Emma won't let anything happen to him. I know she won't." Aunt Gwennie nodded beside her and then put her hand on my shoulder. "Please. We've got this."

Emma stared at Ayla. "What do you mean, you've got this?"

"I'm so sorry, Emma, but we can't really say," Ami said. "We're not really on the same side at the moment."

Emma blinked once, twice. She looked frustrated, uncomfortable, and confused all at once. "Of course we are! If you have evidence to exonerate him, we'll take it, and I'm sure we'll be very grateful to have it."

The police officers glanced back and forth at me, then Emma. Finally, they straightened and moved to get in the car. I guess they could sense nothing would get resolved staring one another down on the lawn. One got into the driver's seat, and the other stood next to the passenger door, his hand on the door handle.

Just in case one of us attacked Emma, no doubt.

Okay, in case I attacked Emma.

"Fine," I said through gritted teeth, then turned to my turncoat best friend. "I'm calling his mother, and she'll no doubt send a lawyer." I glanced into the back seat. "Don't you dare question him without one. Do you hear me? He has a lawyer."

"Okay. Okay." She nodded.

"Fine."

Her eyes softened. "Astra, I'm so sorry," Emma told me quietly. She looked at all of us gathered there, her expression twisted with concern. "Listen, you might not believe this, but I really don't want to arrest him. He has information, though, and I need it. I'm just doing my job. I can't work with you on this, I can't let you near this case—but if you get evidence on your own, get it to me."

I wanted to be angry at her.

Oh, man, did I want to be angry at her.

But I couldn't be.

I'd made a mistake, and I knew it. I'd gotten sidetracked by Aunt Gertie, and I took my eye off the ball. I knew how fast law enforcement could move when it wanted to. What's more, I'd let Jason help out at the shop, so when Emma showed up, he was effectively alone and defenseless. Once he was in cuffs, I had no moves. I was an idiot.

I trusted that Emma would leave Jason alone because of who he was to me.

I should have known better.

I sighed. "I know you don't want to arrest him," I told her. "And I know..." I looked past the police cars to the door of the house. "I know you're just doing your job." I leaned in toward the back window of the police car and met Jason's wide eyes. "We're going to get you out of this."

"I know you will," Jason called loudly through the sealed windows to make sure I heard him. "Don't worry about me. I'll be fine."

Jason…in the back seat of a police car.

It just looked wrong.

I nearly ran into one of the officers as I turned to go back into my house. He reached out a hand to steady me. "I'm sorry," he told me quietly. "If we'd known he was your boyfriend, we'd have talked to you before taking him in." There was sympathy in his eyes.

I didn't remember his name, but I'd seen him around the station before. I glanced at his chest—Officer Diamond.

I nodded and murmured thanks.

Emma knew.

And she didn't call.

I knew why she didn't call, but…it still hurt.

As the car pulled away, my family came toward me. I waved them away, pulled out my phone, and called Jason's mother to let my possible future mother-in-law know that I may have just gotten her son one step closer to being arrested for murder.

* * *

"SO, HERE'S THE THING," I said once we were back inside. "I don't want to hear anything about a tree limb, or some teenage spell gone wrong, or why you two"—I pointed toward Aunt Gwennie and Mom—"lied to us for decades about your sister. All this overly dramatic bull distracted me long enough that Emma just handcuffed my boyfriend and put him in the back of a police car."

"Oh, that's so sweet," Ami murmured.

"What's that?" Aunt Gertie asked.

"Astra called Jason her boyfriend," Althea told the new/old addition to our family. "She tends to have commitment issues," she added with a nod. "She's really fought against labels until—"

"Is this really the time to discuss my romantic life?" I asked in a tone that clarified I didn't care what the answer to the question was, and that it wasn't really a question at all.

"Point taken," Ayla said. "But you're right; this is about more than your love life now."

"What if he really did it?" Aunt Gertie asked. "It's not like the Arden women have a knack for choosing mates that are, shall we say, above board and honest."

"We have excellent taste in men," Aunt

Gwennie told her. "We just tend to make bad choices once we fall in love. It's not the men's fault."

"Sometimes it is absolutely their fault," Aunt Gertie countered. "I told you that spell was not meant to—"

"Gertie," my mother warned. "Don't start."

"But—"

"No," I told them sharply. "I'm done. I'm done with the drama and the intrigue. I'm not going to let Jason go to prison for this. He didn't do it. We're going to find out who really killed Unity Priestpoint. There are seven witches and a magical owl sitting around this table—surely we can suss this out. You all have an eternity to work out this stupid family drama. Jason might have days before the system locks him in a vise grip regardless of his guilt or innocence."

Everyone nodded in agreement.

As much as they would love to spend the entire day hashing out their differences in a gigantic family drum circle, they all knew that I was right.

"You're right, honey," my mother said. "Let's get to work."

CHAPTER NINE

*A*fter I sent Archie to check on Jason, we gathered around the table.

Althea set her laptop in front of her and rested her hands on its keyboard. "Okay, so here's what I found online, right?" Althea announced without raising her eyes from the computer screen. "Unity Priestpoint has two children. Liberty Priestpoint is not Pierre Priestpoint's natural daughter, but he did adopt her after they married."

"They were married eighteen years ago?"

"Yep, that's right."

I frowned and rubbed my chin. Then, a thought came to me. "But wouldn't Liberty have been an adult by then?"

142 | LEANNE LEEDS

Althea nodded. "It was an adult adoption. My guess would be Pierre wanted to make sure Liberty was taken care of along with Gaston when he and Unity both passed away. The adoption just tied up inheritance lines more neatly, I guess."

"Also makes it clear Pierre intended Liberty to inherit, I'd think," Ayla added.

"We can go talk to their lawyer and try to figure out why he did it. Wynn Rogers appears to have been the family lawyer since the beginning. He handled Pierre's estate when he died, and he is Gaston's attorney of record in New York for all of his legal troubles." Thea looked up at me. "He's on everything. He probably knows all the family secrets. Well, if there are any, I mean."

I nodded. "Okay, so that means Gaston is Pierre's natural son?"

"And Liberty's half brother," Althea said. "Though after the adoption, technically, her full brother. Depending on how you look at it, I guess."

"Did Pierre have any other kids from a previous marriage or anything?"

Althea shook her head no. "Not that I was able to find. Pierre and Unity were actually together a lot longer than they were married."

Mom leaned forward. "Just a second. Who's the natural father of Liberty Priestpoint?"

"I wasn't able to find out."

Mom leaned back and looked at Gwennie. "Do you remember what that adoptee you were counseling said about adult adoptions?"

"Oh, you're right, Minnie." Aunt Gwennie turned toward Althea. "I would dig a little deeper on that if you can. Adult adoptions in Florida are very simple, and one of the reasons they're simple is that they don't terminate anyone's parental rights. The adoptee consents to the adoption, and they get a 'new parent' on paper with more rights than they had. However, the old parent *still* has rights of inheritance, rights to challenge."

"So Liberty's birth father could have rights of inheritance?" I asked.

"Yes, he could," Aunt Gwennie said, nodding. "Though that would be a right to inherit from her, not Unity, so I'm not sure that it has anything to do with this."

"We definitely should talk to the lawyer and get the lay of the land, then. And I'd like to go and talk to Liberty Priestpoint, too. I still don't understand why someone would call for a well check on their mother when they live in town and could just pop by," I said with a nod.

"I could go with you," Ayla offered. "Pretend to be one of her students asking about the funeral or something. While we talk to her, Aunt Gertie can look through the house and see if she spots anything suspicious."

I looked at my youngest sister, who, just a day before, would have taken my head off rather than ask me to step to the side in a hallway I was blocking. But, considering her behavior of late, I wasn't entirely sure I could rely on her.

"What? Do I have something on my face?" Ayla wiped her mouth.

I had to admit Ayla did seem more relaxed, more at ease, for the first time in a long time. The tension I'd seen in her shoulders, the tight set of her jaw, had dissipated somewhat. Other than a few glares in Mom's direction, my sister seemed almost centered. This was definitely a change.

"That would help, Ayla."

"I want to help," she said, a little defensively.

I half-smiled. "No one said you didn't want to help."

"You're actually going to let her go on this?" my mother demanded.

I felt instantly defensive of Ayla. "Yes, Mom, I am," I said, with a little more determination than I intended. "I'm going to keep an eye on her, but I think she's serious about wanting to help, and I'm not going to punish her for past sins." I narrowed my eyes. "I would think you of all people might appreciate that attitude toward family right about now."

Mom looked like she was about to say something else, but then she looked down at the table. "That was uncalled for," she muttered under her breath.

"She's trying, right?" I asked.

Mom had to be feeling pretty conflicted right now. On the one hand, she really wanted to rein Ayla in because of the way she'd been acting. But, on the other, Ayla'd been acting the way she was —apparently—as a consequence of things Mom had done.

My mother drew in a sharp breath but said nothing.

"I don't think Astra will have any problem with her, Minnie," Aunt Gwennie said, patting my mother's shoulder. "Ayla might have been a little distracted recently, but she's always had good instincts."

"A little distracted?" Mom asked sharply.

"*What* did I say about the drama?" I asked her, my stare sharp and my eyes cold. "Jason's in trouble. Put a cork in it until we deal with it."

She straightened and nodded. "Yes. Sorry, dear. I didn't mean anything by it."

"Good, because I need all hands on deck with this investigation. No distractions. We really don't know what's going on yet," I said, standing up and stretching my back. "Althea, get back to the computer. Try to find out anything you can on Gaston and Liberty. First, I'll talk to the lawyer and see how much he'll give up. Then we'll head over to Liberty's."

"Your mother and I will keep trying to figure out what the deal is with that trunk," Aunt Gwennie told me. Then she frowned. "It would be much more helpful if we had it."

"I can get it for you—" Ayla began, but I stopped her.

"No," I said firmly before Ayla could propose stealing evidence from my employer. "We can't translocate evidence from the police station. Emma was right. This is a human murder case— at least as far as we know right now—and we can't break any laws like that. But, she and I do have an agreement, and for now, I'm going to keep to it."

"For now?" Ami asked, eyebrow raised.

"Jason didn't do this, and if it's in my power to stop it, I will," I told her. "Sometimes, my power falls a little bit outside of the law, but we'll cross that bridge when we come to it."

* * *

AYLA AND I walked into the strip mall legal office of Wynn Rogers with some surprise. It was a small room with no receptionist. The walls were covered in cheap paneling, and there was a desk in the corner with a computer and a phone.

Wynn Rogers was sitting behind the desk, typing on the computer. He looked up when we came in, an expression of wary surprise on his face. "Can I help you?"

Ayla and I exchanged a puzzled look. This guy was the lawyer for a pretty wealthy couple—by all accounts, he handled all of the Priestpoints' legal work. We hadn't expected the office to be so small or shoddy.

Wynn Rogers didn't stand up to greet us. He had a deep tan that made his skin look dry and leathery, one of those older Florida folks that seemed to think skin cancer was a goal. The lawyer had brown eyes and a crooked nose that looked like it'd been broken a time or two. I noticed he wasn't wearing a wedding ring.

"We'd like to speak to you about Gaston and

Liberty Priestpoint. Ask a few questions, if I could," I told him, taking a seat. "I'm Astra. This is my sister Ayla."

"I'm sorry, but the Priestpoints are no longer my clients. And I'm not sure what you mean by speak to me." Wynn Rogers cleared his throat, and I noticed for the first time he was dressed up, shirt and tie and slacks—the outfit was higher dollar than the office. "What is this about?" He stared closer. "Wait a minute, aren't you that psychic woman that works for the police department? The one that's been in the paper?"

"I am, in fact, that woman," I told him, my smile wide as if his recognizing me was just the most flattering thing in the world. (I *was* actually pretty pleased about it. It kept me from implying we were here on official police business. Which was probably against the law—since I wasn't. One less felony to worry about.) "I wanted to ask you about Unity Priestpoint. I imagine you've heard by now that she passed away this morning."

"No, I hadn't heard that," he responded. His face was impassive. Wynn Rogers either didn't care that someone he knew died, or he'd been informed already and what I said wasn't a surprise. "Unity and I haven't had much to do with each other for some time. So where did she pass away?"

Where.

Where did she pass away.

Not how.

Not when.

Where.

"She was found in her bedroom this morning," I told him.

"How sad. I did know that she was getting on in years, but she was a good woman." The lawyer frowned deeply as if attempting to remember something essential but then sighed and said, "I fail to see what this has to do with me."

While he spoke, the man was fiddling with paperwork on his desk.

And it was...odd.

The lawyer would look down briefly, look up, meet my gaze, and then reach down without looking to stack one piece of paper on top of another. Again and again, the same pattern. It was almost hypnotic.

"The circumstances surrounding her death are a little suspicious," I continued. "I'd like to ask a few questions that might help us, if you don't mind. Since you were so intimately involved with the family for such a long time."

"I'm sorry, but I'm quite busy," Rogers told me, standing. He shoved the paperwork into a drawer and locked it, then picked up another stack of files. "I've got to be somewhere right now. I don't have time for idle chatter."

Wynn Rogers didn't seem to care much about the death of a woman he'd once taken on as a client and had known for years.

"This isn't exactly idle. The police are investigating her death as a possible murder," I told him. "They're looking into all of her relationships, and no offense, but you're on that list." Again, not so much as a vaguely surprised look from the strip mall lawyer when I mentioned murder.

"What sorts of relationships?" Wynn Rogers asked.

"I'm not really at liberty to discuss that," I told him in my best Emma voice.

"I see." He was studying me, his eyes steady and unblinking, like a lizard's. "Look, I have to go. I'm sorry I can't help you."

I stood up, and Ayla followed. "Of course. Thank you for your time."

"I'll walk you out," Rogers told me. He stood against his desk and moved directly toward us like he was herding cattle. He followed us all the way out into the strip mall parking lot. Then he followed us all the way to my Jeep and stood beside me expectantly, waiting for us to get in.

Seriously?

I didn't like the feeling I was getting from him, a feeling that grew the longer I was around him— it made me think of snakes and alligators and predatory eyes that never seemed to blink.

In a much more friendly tone, Wynn Rogers said, "Well, again, I'm sorry, but I can't help you. I'm due in court in two hours, and I need to prepare. However, I do want to say that if Liberty or Gaston were suspected of anything, they couldn't have done it. They loved their mother very much and never would have hurt her."

I stared at him.

What an unbelievably odd thing to say.

"Sure," I told him as I clambered in the Jeep. I closed the door and stuck my head out of the open window. "Thank you for your time."

"Just to be clear, I didn't give you my time," Wynn responded shortly. Wynn Rogers stood there for a moment, still staring at me. Then, a second later, he turned around, walked back into his office, and closed the door—as if forgetting he'd just told us he had somewhere to be.

"What was *that* about?" Ayla asked me.

"I don't know, but I'm not so sure I like it," I told her as I rolled up my window.

"I didn't like him," she said. "He gave me the creeps."

Maybe Rogers was just a genuinely cold and uncaring person—the kind of guy that would have such a narrow view of the world it wouldn't occur to him to be upset about the death of a client he served for many years.

But I didn't think that was the case.

There was something else going on.

I put the Jeep into gear and hit the gas. "Let's find out where he's due in court and for what," I told Ayla. "Call Althea and have her let Aunt Gwennie know we're heading to Liberty's after visiting the courthouse."

BEFORE GOING over to Liberty Priestpoint's house, I wanted to look at Rogers's court calendar. Ayla and I exchanged a few words with a clerk who did, in fact, know Wynn Rogers and was happy to share his day's agenda and a printout of all the cases he was working on.

It was...quite puzzling.

Two months ago, Wynn Rogers only handled

cases for the Priestpoints. Liberty, Unity, Gaston —they'd all had various civil cases here and there that he appeared for. Then, seven weeks ago, Wynn Rogers suddenly took random clients as if he'd thrown up a shingle as a lawyer for the first time in his life.

Was he doing his best to distance himself from his ex-client? And if so, was it deliberate? Had he been fired, or was it an elaborate cover-up to make it look like he was no longer associated with the Priestpoint family?

We discovered Wynn Rogers wasn't lying about needing to be in court that day. He was handling a case for another lawyer, an elderly man named Lester Cooper. Cooper and his ex-wife were arguing over a divorce settlement. The previous Mrs. Cooper wanted a cash payment of $1.5 million, but Lester wanted to give her three-hundred acres of land in Lockney, Texas.

"Astra, what are you doing at the courthouse?"

When I looked up, Detective Emma Sullivan was staring at me in the hallway outside the clerk's office. "Ayla's thinking about going into the legal profession," I said with a shrug as I rolled Rogers's paperwork into a tight scroll so it couldn't be seen. "I thought I'd take her on a field trip to a courthouse." I turned to Ayla. "Are you learning something?"

Ayla nodded. "Absolutely. It's great preparation for the future. This is all very exciting."

"I see." Detective Sullivan's eyes flicked from me to Ayla, then back. "You know I don't believe either one of you, right?"

"You should have a more open mind," I told her.

"I should trust my instincts. And my gut tells me you're here because you're spying on Wynn Rogers," she said. "You think he might be involved in Unity's death."

I thought about lying to her, making up some reason we were there that had nothing to do with the retired teacher, her death, or my boyfriend's current incarceration, but what was the point?

Emma knew me well enough to know I wasn't going to leave it alone.

"Yeah, okay, but we didn't *spy*. We walked right into his office," I told her, crossing my arms. "I could be wrong, but there's something way off about that guy. He claims he's not Unity's lawyer anymore. Okay, sure. But when I told him she was dead? He didn't ask me how or when it happened. He just wanted to know where she was found. It was totally hinky."

"I know what I'm about to say is going to be as effective as banging my head against the wall, but I want you to leave the investigation to the police. Which, today, is not you."

"I wish I could."

"I mean it, Astra. This is a total conflict of interest for you. I'm not going to let you—"

"In all the time we've known each other, when have you ever known anyone to let me or not let me do anything? Seriously, Sullivan, let it drop. When have I ever let anyone else control my actions? You're embarrassing yourself with your own naive expectations." I waved her off. "You can arrest me later if you want."

"Astra!"

"Bye, Detective Sullivan."

Ayla and I turned and started walking back down the hall, but we didn't get very far. The detective caught up with us, took hold of my arm, and swiveled me around.

"Where exactly are you going?" Emma's eyes shifted to Ayla. "And where are you taking your kid sister? She shouldn't be around all this. This is an actual murder investigation. That means there's an actual murderer."

"Okay, look." I shook my head, holding out my hands to stop her from talking. "The woman was found in a trunk covered with magical symbols that messed with my psychometry. Maybe a plain old bullet ended her life, but there's magic in this case."

"Do you know that for—"

"So, from my perspective, *my* rules probably apply—not yours," I continued without letting her get a sentence in. "Now, I'm willing to follow your lead on most things, and I'm going to do my best not to screw up your case, but you have Jason Bishop in a *cell*, Emma. A cell. Like a criminal. Quit telling me to back off," I told her as bluntly as I could. "It's not going to happen, and you know it. And if you were me and the situation was reversed, you wouldn't either."

Emma's eyes blazed, and she pursed her lips. She wanted to argue with me and come up with something that would make me stand aside.

But in the end, she couldn't.

Instead, Emma glanced over my shoulder toward the other cops in the hallway and leaned in. "If you're determined to stick your nose in this, I'll do my best to give you a wide berth so the captain doesn't catch you," she told me in a low voice. "But Astra, so help me, you have to protect the case. And you have to keep me informed."

"I know that. I will. Right now, the hinky lawyer's weird behavior is pretty much all I know for sure." I decided to keep the maid's information to myself for now. Nothing she said rang alarm bells for me, and Emma would find her on her own through routine police work. I glanced at my phone. "We have to get going."

I could see the struggle on my friend's face. She wanted to push me, but she couldn't find a good enough reason. So instead, she asked casually, "Oh? Where are you going, and what are you looking for?"

I chuckled. "For a detective, you can be really transparent sometimes. Look, you need to check into the lawyer. All I can tell you is something is hinky there," I explained. Then, as a gesture of goodwill, I handed her the case history and outlined, briefly, what transpired at his office and what we found on his schedule. "We're going to Liberty's now. My aunt is meeting us there. I want to look around."

"You don't have a search warrant."

"No. I have a ghost. It's better than a search warrant."

CHAPTER TEN

We were in the Jeep just a few moments when Ayla turned to me and said, "I don't understand how Mom could do that to her own sister. I can't even imagine doing something like that to you or Ami or Thea. And I can't understand how you're taking this all so calmly."

"Do what?" I asked, my eyes on the road. "Ban her ghost from the house and everyone's view?"

"Yeah."

"It could have been worse," I told her.

"How?"

"I heard a story back in Impy about a ghost who'd been imprisoned in a watch fob," I explained as I turned onto Main Street. "When they got him out, he was insane. I mean, okay, he was stuck in an object and not in the real world. So, expected, right? Anyway, once freed, he just flew around saying 'tick, tick, tick.'"

"By his family? He was put in there by them, too?"

"Well," I glanced over at her. "No. It wasn't done by family."

"I don't know." Ayla shrugged. "I can't believe Mom did that. It's not right, in my opinion. It's not right. Aunt Gertie was a good person, wasn't she?"

"Was she?" I asked seriously, stopping at a light and turning to Ayla. "Mom and Aunt Gwennie both seemed pretty insistent that she *wasn't* a very good person when she was alive." I heard my sister's quick intake of breath before I saw it and held up my hand to stop her barrage of protestation. "Before you argue, I must state that her influence on you over the last few months has not been positive. That attitude wasn't a good place to start if you wanted to argue her case." The light turned green, and I accelerated as I turned away. "I'm not taking Mom's side here, but I am holding my judgment in reserve on Aunt Gertie until I have more information."

Ayla paused for a moment and then said, "Aunt Gertie said that's quite fair and reasonable."

I half-smiled. "Did she, now?"

"Yes." Pause. "She said that she was thrilled to hear that. She said she'd like to be part of our family, but if we don't want her around after getting to know her, she understands." Another pause. "She said that if you think it's best if she goes away, she doesn't mind. But if she goes," Ayla added quickly, "frankly, I go, too."

"Ayla, let's not jump the gun here. No one's going anywhere just yet." Except maybe Jason, who might wind up in Gainesville doing life for murdering an old colleague. "I'm just saying your behavior's really been beyond the pale the last few months. I understand you were angry at Mom because of what Aunt Gertie told you, but you should've come to Ami or me or Thea with what was happening."

"We were afraid you'd say we were crazy like Mom did," she mumbled.

"But you weren't. And we would have believed you."

"Really? But—" Ayla seemed to hesitate, as though struck by the idea. "You're probably right. I'm sorry," she said quietly.

"It's okay. But for future reference, instead of

trying to take my head off when I ask you what's wrong, you could have just asked me if I knew Mom had another sister. You could have asked any of us. We would have told you if we knew anything about it. Instead, you didn't even give us a chance."

When I finished, she was silent for a long moment. Finally, I glanced over, and she met my eyes. "Fine. I should have probably come to you guys and not assumed you were lying to me the way she was lying to me. But this doesn't mean I'm changing my mind about Mom," she said with a stubborn set to her jaw. "I don't think it's right, what she did. And maybe even worse, I don't think it's right she lied to all of us." She turned toward the back seat. "No, I know it's not worse. But you know what I mean."

"I have to admit I'm with you there," I told Ayla as we pulled onto Liberty Priestpoint's street. "I'm not saying it is right or better or worse than what Gertie went through," I told her, "but I do think coming to me or Ami or Thea would have been the right thing to do. You know, before you turned into *l'enfant terrible*."

"Family secrets are nasty things," Ayla said with a shudder. "I wonder if that's why that lady got killed. We seem to be talking a whole lot about her family. Do you think she had secrets?"

"Everybody has secrets, Ayla," I told her sincerely. "And sometimes they're secret for a reason, and it's okay. But sometimes people's secrets poison everything around them until something has to give."

"Like the dead lady."

"Yup."

* * *

I PULLED up in front of the house and put the car in park.

It was a modest two-story house in a neighborhood of modest two-story houses—in other words, it didn't scream "I have rich parents." As I shut off the engine, I could hear the hum of the freeway in the distance, but here it was quiet. "Now, let's go and see what we can find out about Liberty Priestpoint. Remember, Ayla," I told her quietly, "this woman just lost her mother this morning. You have to give grieving people a pretty wide birth to be addled."

She nodded. "What do you want Aunt Gertie to do?"

"Just look around inside the house. Since she can move without being seen, she can go through the bedrooms and see if anything jumps out. Papers. A gun laying out. A suitcase indicating she's about to leave town. Anything that seems wrong."

Ayla looked to the side, her eyes focused on something I couldn't see. "Aunt Gertie said she understands."

I nodded and looked up at the house, mentally steeling myself.

To be frank, dealing with hyper-emotional people wasn't exactly in my wheelhouse. I was kind of like lava, sort of—hard, distant, and steady most of the time. So solid you could climb on it and be reasonably confident it would support you.

But rarely, I could become a glowing and flowing seething river of molten fury. When that happens? Get the hell out of my way, or I will run you over.

But lava, in all of its forms, was far from soothing.

As soon as I extended a leg toward the house, the front door opened.

I could see Liberty Priestpoint through the screen, and the resemblance between her and her mother was unmistakable. Her silvery-brown hair was highlighted by her black dress, which she wore on a slender frame. The woman's pale, slightly lined complexion was splotchy, and the smudges under her eyes were large black circles, indicating that she had been crying.

Despite the tragedy surrounding her, she'd done her hair. It was short and spiky and curved nicely around her face. She looked good for her age, the strands of gray hair giving Liberty gravitas as opposed to highlighting her nearly fifty years.

"Hello, Ms. Priestpoint," I said, stopping at the bottom of the steps. "May we come in?" I didn't introduce myself or explain why we were there.

She looked at us through the screen door with suspicion at first, but after a moment, opened it slightly. Within seconds, a younger man appeared next to her out of nowhere and pulled the screen door closed with a bang.

His dark brown hair was a bit long, his brown eyes a little sunken, but he held himself with a kind of arrogant grace. I wondered if it was her husband or brother.

If husband, go her—the guy couldn't have been a day over thirty-five.

"My name is Gaston Priestpoint," the man

said. "I'm Liberty's brother. Who are you, and what do you want on today of all days?"

I would have guessed he was in his mid-thirties, though I knew from his file he was only twenty-nine. Nearly twenty years older, Liberty was a much smaller woman than her brother and he towered over her. Gaston's stance felt more defensive than protective of his sister, but I couldn't have told you precisely why I felt that way.

His proximity seemed to make Liberty tense.

Or, well, maybe that was me.

"I've been working with Detective Emma Sullivan at the Forkbridge Police Department," I told Gaston, being as truthful as I could without outright lying about what I was doing there. "I let her know I'd be stopping by to talk to your sister. Since you're here, you'll save me a trip to talk to you."

There.

Implication turned all the way up, but no outright lie.

"Do the police often bring children with them?" Gaston asked, his tone snotty.

"Ayla is my assistant today. Kind of a 'bring your daughter to work' day thing," I told him with a nonchalant shrug. "If you'd like her to wait in the car, I can leave her there, but it's a bit hot out today."

It was Florida. It was a bit hot out almost every day.

Liberty reached out and put a thin hand on her brother's arm. "What is this about, Miss...?"

"My name is Astra Arden and—"

"You're that psychic witch with the police department!" Gaston said, alarmed. "I saw you on that television show, that news at ten feature. You find lost things or something." He narrowed his eyes. "We've lost nothing but our mother, and we know exactly where she is. In the morgue."

Well. A little blunt.

Maybe even sociopathically blunt.

"I'm a psychic consultant, yes," I corrected him, finding psychic witch a bit redundant. "I'd like to come in and ask you a few questions."

"About my mother?" Liberty asked, puzzled. I nodded, watching her closely. "They arrested the man that shot her, they said. Or someone that knows who shot her." She closed her eyes and took a deep breath, then swallowed. "I'm sorry, I'm having a difficult time keeping it all straight in my—"

"Did my mother send you?" he asked, glaring at me as if I would demand he accompany me to the dentist for a root canal. Gaston puffed, his breaths short and slightly frantic. "Is that why you're here? One of those Cassandra charlatans that prey on the weak after a catastrophe to get money? You know our mother was wealthy, don't you? Is that why you're here?" His gaze stabbed me like a knife as he cracked his knuckles ominously.

It didn't bother me. Barky men staring out from behind screen doors didn't scream "be worried"—if he was really someone to be concerned about, he would have stepped out in front of the door. *That* action would have protected the home from entry and defended his sister from attack.

I mean, if I was intending to attack.

Which I wasn't.

This was fortunate for Liberty. I had a feeling her hulking brother, despite his size, was a largely ineffective defense strategy.

Gaston, in my opinion, was just a bully.

His reaction *did* pique my curiosity, though. Which one of his rapid-fire questions really concerned him? That his mother's ghost may have sent me, or that I was after his money? Why even ask if his dear departed mother sent me? Where did that question come from?

And…did he believe in ghosts?

Because if he did, he likely believed in all sorts of other magic things…

…like wooden chests that put psychic powers on the fritz.

My sister leaned over and poked me in the ribs as I thought about all of this. "Astra," Ayla whispered, pointing toward a butterfly that hovered just to the right of the door. "Astra, that's my butterfly."

The butterfly's wings were cerulean blue with orange and gold splotches on the edges. It flitted from one side of the threshold to the other as if trying to persuade Liberty and Gaston to let it in, too.

"What do you mean, 'your butterfly?'" Liberty asked, frowning slightly.

"A butterfly? What do you think that is, some kind of a sign?" Gaston scoffed at his sister, then twisted his head to glare at me. "Off limits," Gaston said, pointing at me with one of his large, sinewy hands. "I don't want you talking to her." His gaze focused on me with a kind of concentration that might have made someone feel uncomfortable.

Not me.

But, you know, someone.

"Liberty, I'd just like to ask you a few—"

"Yeah?" Gaston clenched and unclenched his fists. "What business is it of yours? If you have any questions, go see our lawyer. That's why we pay the man." He looked like he would explode, and his sister put a hand on his arm.

"Gaston, please. I don't understand why you're getting so upset with—"

"Liberty," he said, his voice deepening. "This is a private matter. We don't know these people, and they have no reason to be here. The police arrested Arthur Dallas for the murder, and that's all that there is to it—"

"Arthur Dallas?" I asked, frowning. "Who is—"

"Get off our property!" Gaston said fiercely. "Talk to our lawyer, Wynn Rogers. If we need to talk to you, he'll let us know. But, until then, leave."

With that, Gaston yanked his older sister back from the screen and slammed the door.

The small, bright blue butterfly flew toward the barred entry and flapped around in front of it, its wings moving faster than before. (Honestly, if a butterfly could flap angrily, that's what it looked like it was doing.) Finally, it landed on the door, perched on the screen, and waited.

For what? I had no idea.

I didn't think Gaston Priestpoint would let the butterfly in any more than he let Ayla and me in. "You may want to tell the butterfly to wait around back if you can," I told my sister before we turned around to walk away. "I have a feeling Gaston may come back out here with a fly swatter."

* * *

"So, I have questions."

Of course she did. I started the Jeep and said, "Shoot."

"Okay. So. The butterfly was trying to tell us something when it appeared in front of the screen door, I think," Ayla said thoughtfully. "Do you think it wanted us to talk to Arthur Dallas? Or do you think Unity Priestpoint—her soul, I mean—is in her daughter's house?"

"It's your butterfly, Ayla. You'd know better than I would what it was trying to say. But, if you don't know, that might be a better question for Aunt Gertie," I admitted. "Is she back?"

"No, not yet." Ayla turned to me with a quizzical look on her face. "Who is Arthur Dallas?"

She *would* follow up with that one. I'd never heard the name before.

As soon as we were out of sight of the house, I turned down a cross street and parked the Jeep in a shady spot beneath a large tree. "No idea. But while we wait for Aunt Gertie, we can call Emma and see if we can find out," I told her. I took out my phone and dialed Emma, then pressed the speaker button so Ayla could hear.

She noticed and looked pleased.

"Yo," Emma said abruptly. "What's up?"

"Ayla and I just left Liberty Priestpoint's place. Or, to be more accurate, Liberty's front porch. Her brother, Gaston, was there, and neither one of them would let us in—though I think Liberty would have if Gaston hadn't been there barking at us like a junkyard dog."

"Yeah, he's a real charmer, isn't he?"

"So, I have two things," I said, shifting in the seat. "One, Gaston claimed Arthur Dallas had been arrested for Unity's murder. Who's Arthur Dallas, and have you guys arrested him?"

Emma's pause was long and ominous. "No, Arthur Dallas has not been arrested. He's Unity's next door neighbor. But, honestly, we weren't even looking into him as a person of interest." Another pause. "When I talked to him, I told him —Gaston—we had a person of interest in custody, but I didn't say who." Another pause.

"And, you know, now that I think about it, he didn't ask who."

"Person of interest?" Ayla repeated. "What does that mean?"

"Hey, there, Ayla," Emma said. "That means that we're not actively pursuing someone to arrest them, but we think they could be involved in the crime, so they're on our radar."

"So Arthur Dallas is not in custody?" Ayla asked.

"Nope. Only Jason Bishop, and he's only being held as a material witness for now."

Ayla raised her eyebrow. "Okay, and what does that mean?"

"That you should be watching more *Law and Order* with Althea," Emma joked.

"That means, Ayla, that the police believe he has important information and may flee with it, so they're holding him to ensure he doesn't," I told her. "But what it really means is that they want to arrest Jason but don't have enough evidence, so they're going to keep him in jail until they do or a lawyer forces them to release him."

"Well, that doesn't seem right," Ayla said with a frown.

"I don't make the laws, Ayla," Emma replied in a matter-of-fact tone. "I simply enforce them and take advantage of any loopholes provided by the Florida state legislature to make my job easier and the criminals' jobs more challenging. On this loophole thing, by the way, your big sister is usually right there with me."

I rolled my eyes. "Usually, we're chasing actual criminals and not my boyfriend."

"Again, he's not under arrest. His criminality has yet to be determined. And by the way, smooth move sending Archie to keep an eye on him," Emma said in a slightly indignant tone. "Your gigantic, menacing owl is scaring the hell out of the guards. A new guy already quit."

I smiled but said nothing.

"Didn't you have another thing to tell Emma?" Ayla asked. "You said two things."

"Oh, right," I nodded. "So, I talked to Wynn earlier today, right? And he told me he wasn't the Priestpoints' lawyer anymore. Like, for any of them."

"But Gaston just said that he was!" Ayla said, surprise in her voice.

"And that was the weird part," I said toward the phone. "Gaston claims that Wynn Rogers is their lawyer. He told me specifically that he didn't have anything to do with the Priestpoints anymore and said none of this had anything to do with him—but if he's still the kids' lawyer, that's not true at all."

"So, they lied," Emma said.

"Or he lied," I countered.

"Why can't people just tell the truth to the police?" Emma muttered.

"Because they're criminals?"

In Florida, it was officially a criminal offense for a person to knowingly give false information to law enforcement about the commission of a crime.

But no one was ever prosecuted for it, not really.

And everyone slightly sketchy did it anyway—lying to the police was a first offense misdemeanor with penalties of up to one year in jail or twelve months of probation and a thousand dollar fine.

Punishment for murder? Let me just point out Ted Bundy murdered his way across multiple states. Do you know who executed the guy?

Florida.

So, yeah. Most criminals opted to lie and take their chances.

"Can't a lawyer be disbarred for lying to police?" Ayla asked.

"For lying to *police*," Emma said. "Not the police crystal ball reader."

"I'm not a crystal ball reader," I deadpanned.

"No, you're a pseudo-detective without a badge," she said. "Try not to forget that. The last time you did, you almost lost your job."

"Quit nitpicking. It's not like you're not always up my...uh, looking over my shoulder," I said, my voice taking on a slightly pained tone. "Now, what do you know about Arthur Dallas?"

"Why?"

"We're visiting him next. Tell me everything you know."

CHAPTER ELEVEN

I was surprised by how quiet the neighborhood was when I returned to Unity Priestpoint's home. I would have expected five or six police cars parked in front of the house, their lights flashing and the officers debriefing.

Instead, there was just a single squad car next to the curb. Its headlights were turned off, and the officer within reclined, his head arched back as if inspecting the inner roof of his vehicle.

In Orlando, there might have been five police cars, a news van, and a hundred people roped off, hoping to glimpse something terrible to tell the neighbors who weren't fortunate enough to witness the drama.

Here?

Nope.

It was nap time at the Priestpoint residence.

Well…former residence.

Arthur Dallas's house sat just to the right of the crime-scene-taped Priestpoint home. It was an impressive beige stucco house with a meticulously mowed square of green grass in the front, a concrete patio with a tall tree off the side, and a white Lexus parked in the driveway.

A thick-trunked oak tree rose up behind the house, its branches bare and reaching high into the sky, as if it were grasping for something just beyond its fingertips. I suspected that tree was the scene of Archie's snooping. I breathed in, and the smell of freshly cut grass filled the air.

Ayla and I walked along the sidewalk, looking back at the Priestpoints' house every few steps. I could see nothing that might have obscured Arthur Dallas's (or Archie's) view of Unity's house. The Priestpoint driveway ran directly between the two homes, turning sharply to the left and disappearing at the back of the house.

Dallas's patio on the left side of his house (thanks to his L-shaped backyard) had a perfect view of Unity's comings and goings if he decided to monitor them. And, let's face it, considering this was Forkbridge, I had a better than average shot at getting a nosy neighbor.

I rang the doorbell.

The door was answered by a fifty-something woman dressed in a purple tracksuit. Her broad, weathered face was framed by her thick, graying hair. Just behind her appeared a young man in his late twenties or early thirties with a thin face, shaggy hair, and a scruffy goatee. He was dressed in a baseball cap and red shorts. His oversized black t-shirt said, "CONSPIRACY THEORY EXPERT: Ask Me Anything."

Okay, then.

"Hi, my name is Astra Arden, and this is my sister, Ayla," I told the two, wondering briefly what it was about this town and women not answering the door by themselves. "I work for the Forkbridge Police Department, and I was hoping to talk to Arthur Dallas about Unity Priestpoint." I paused and waited. Nothing. "I'm sure you've heard she was found dead early this morning?"

Truth, but not the whole truth.

Without answering, the woman stepped back as if to invite me in.

"Thank you so much." I smiled and stepped forward.

"Did somebody say you could come in?" she asked. Her expression was curious, but her tone was the same one the police used to verbally inform you of the limits of your rights. "Why do you want to talk to Arthur?" I opened my mouth to answer, but before I could, the woman glanced at her neighbor's house, made a face, and said, "Just a minute." She shut the door.

"Okay, weird," Ayla said in a low tone. "Aunt Gertie went in already. She said he's there. Three people."

A moment later, the door opened again, and the woman impatiently waved us in.

The woman (who had yet to introduce herself) pointed to a man just inside the door. He was tall, skinny, and balding, dressed casually in a shirt and jeans, but his body language suggested a man in charge.

The woman turned. "This is Arthur."

"Are you going to arrest him?" the younger man behind her asked. The question was delivered in a breathy voice, with a pitch higher than a man's typical tone—almost like he forced lightheartedness. The voice didn't go with his stern expression or the harsh lines of his face.

I shook my head. "No. I work for the FPD, but

I'm not a police officer. I'm a consultant, and I just wanted to ask some questions."

There. Again.

Truth, but not the whole truth.

The woman looked back and forth between us, then shrugged and turned around, gesturing for us to follow her deeper into the house. "Go on into the kitchen. I have a Zoom meeting, and the last thing I need is for my coworkers to see that the town psychic witch person is poking about my house. It's bad enough that horrible woman died here instead of a hospital like a proper southern woman."

I'm sure the proper southern way to die was precisely what was on her mind as someone pointed a gun at her head.

Sheesh.

"I apologize for my wife," the balding man I assumed was Arthur Dallas told me. His tone was friendly but very matter-of-fact. "She tends to get stressed out easily. Her job moved to the other side of the country several years ago, but we couldn't follow." The woman's eyes flashed with anger. "She also has a tendency to speak without thinking first." Purple tracksuit stormed out of the hallway and into the adjacent room toward the right of us, her face red with anger.

I felt a pang of regret I wasn't interviewing her. People that speak without thinking first are the best people to interrogate.

"Why don't you follow me into the kitchen so we don't bother Millie, and we can all talk," he said.

Ayla and I followed him into an airy kitchen. The young man in the conspiracy theory t-shirt was following when I looked behind me.

* * *

DALLAS POINTED at two chairs in front of a wicker table. The table, reasonably large with six additional chairs, sat next to a large bay window overlooking the patio—and Unity Priestpoint's home. The driveway and the front door were clearly visible from the kitchen. "Please, sit down. Can I get you something to drink?"

"No, thanks. By the way, you *are* Arthur Dallas, correct? I know your wife said so, but I just want to formally confirm."

He looked slightly embarrassed and then nodded. "Yes. I'm sorry, I didn't introduce myself." He pointed toward the baseball cap conspiracy theory guy. "That's my son, Jody."

Jody nodded silently and took a seat across

from Ayla. He scowled at me, his gaze full of suspicion.

"And your wife is Millie?" Ayla asked. Before Dallas could answer, Ayla added, "I'm Ayla Arden, by the way."

"Hello, Ayla. Yes," Dallas nodded. "Millie is my wife. And you can call me Artie. Everyone does." The balding man grabbed a glass, filled it with ice, and opened the refrigerator to pull out a pitcher of light yellow liquid. "Are you sure you don't want anything to drink? We have fresh-squeezed lemonade."

I shook my head no. "No, thank you again. Do you have any idea why I might have come to talk to you?" I've found that giving suspects a wide runway to land on sometimes uncovered things far faster than targeted questions.

Jody's eyes darted from me to his father to Ayla and back again.

"Not a clue." Dallas's expression suggested he was puzzled, but he spoke in a tone of voice that was as pleasant as lemon meringue pie. "Well, I know Unity passed away, and she was found this morning. But beyond that, no."

"I wanted to ask you a few questions about Unity."

He nodded, then said, "Logical. Of course,

please. I'd like to be as helpful as I can. She and I didn't always get along because of the issues with the oak tree, but all in all, she was a decent woman. We just couldn't come to an agreement about it."

Artie Dallas was pleasant, polite, and charming. Still, he was too smart to volunteer too much information to an open-ended question. "I'll get back to the tree. But, first, I was wondering if you saw or heard anything unusual last night or this morning."

Artie looked like he was just about to answer in a calm, rational voice with a calm, rational answer when his son, Jody, exploded.

The son's eyebrows arched so far up his forehead they almost disappeared. Then, with a swift movement, he scraped his chair back and stood up. "This is ridiculous. I don't know how you people get away with these sorts of things, but this is the most appalling invasion of privacy we've ever had to endure."

Ayla and I looked at each other, baffled. Finally, I turned back to Jody and blinked. "Sorry?"

"You should be!" he said, slamming his hands down on the table.

"No, I mean, 'sorry' as in I have no idea what on earth you're talking about."

Jody's face flushed red like an apple as he turned toward his father. "You should know better than to talk to them without an attorney present!"

"Jody, that's enough," Artie said, sounding exhausted. He pinched the bridge of his nose and closed his eyes. "Please, try and control—"

"No, it's not enough!" Jody's eyes were wide, his nostrils flared, and his hands were in fists, held in tight against his body. His voice had risen to a shout, and he was shaking.

"Jody, please." Artie looked apologetic, but he didn't seem surprised by his son's outburst. "Not in front of our guests, please. Just take a deep breath and calm down. They're just doing their job, and we have nothing to hide." His voice was soft and steely at the same time.

"Why are you so calm?" Jody asked his father. "How can you sit there so calmly? You're a suspect in a murder case! They didn't come here this morning, but I knew they would show up. Knew it! I know things! I know more things than you, you dimwit!"

"I'm sorry," I said, apologizing again for... something. Ayla looked at me, confusion writ large across her face. "But I never said your father was a suspect in anything. You're Unity Priestpoint's neighbors, so I came over to ask some questions, but no one is a suspect in—"

"Why didn't you just get rid of the gun in your nightstand before the police came over?" Jody shouted, his face red and his voice clearly conveying he was on the verge of tears. He pointed a finger at his father. "Do you think they won't find it? Do you really think they won't?" Tears welled up in his eyes as he spoke, and his lip quivered. "You're such an idiot, Dad!"

Apparently, Jody inherited his mother's inability to shut up.

I blinked, leaning back in my chair far enough to get a better look at the son. Jody was pacing around the kitchen like a boxer in a ring. The young man kept opening his mouth to say something else, but then he would shake his head, close his mouth, and continue pacing.

Artie looked at me, his face pained. He looked sad. Maybe even embarrassed.

But he didn't look scared.

Or guilty.

"I sincerely apologize for my son's behavior. He's had some issues the past few years, and we've tried to get him help, but—"

Jody's face twisted and contorted as he glared at his father, his lips twitching. "I have problems? You mean you have problems. You. And it's your gun, isn't it?"

"Jody, please!" Artie pleaded.

"Mr. Dallas, please sit down," I spoke forcefully enough that my voice echoed off the kitchen walls, and electricity sparked faintly in my hands.

Jody whirled toward me, fists clenched. "I don't have any reason to sit down! What are you going to do? Shoot me?" He laughed—the sound a cross between a hiccup and a sob. "Or torture me? Like you did to them? I heard what you did to the vampires! I heard! Are you going to torture me?"

He stormed out of the kitchen and out of the house, slamming the patio door behind him so hard the walls of the large house seemed to rattle.

* * *

Artie sighed and then glanced at us. "I don't know what to say," he said. He looked sad and pained, and I felt a growing sense of unease.

I didn't want to believe that Artie Dallas had killed his neighbor...but his son's outburst

LEEDS

suggested this family had a solid connection to the case that no one seemed to know about yet.

"It's okay. To be honest, I've seen worse," I joked (inappropriately). "I do have to ask you about the gun that Jody mentioned, Artie." I looked at the dejected father. "Do you have a gun in your nightstand? Or any guns at all?"

"We're not a gun family," Artie said with a shake of his head. "Considering the issues Jody's been having, it would be insane for us to bring something like that in this house. So no, Astra, we do not. I assure you there are no guns here. I'd be happy to show you the nightstand," he said, then shook his head sadly. "It must be another one of Jody's fantasies."

I believed Arthur Dallas. My instinct told me he was telling me the truth. I could sense no subterfuge in him, no intent to deceive. He displayed none of the telltale "I'm lying to you" signs I usually look for. And yet...

Something also told me in his nightstand, there was a gun.

Not just a gun.

The gun.

"That would be great, Artie. Showing me, I mean."

Artie motioned toward the doorway that Jody

had stormed through. "I really am sorry. It's been hard on Jody, and he doesn't always... communicate well. He lives in a fantasy world that...anyway, I just want to apologize—"

"It's fine, sir. Where is your nightstand?" I asked to bring him back to the subject at hand. Then, I turned to Ayla and pointed down, indicating she should stay here. Not only did I not want her near any gun we might find, but I also wanted to give her a moment alone to consult with Aunt Gertie.

She nodded silently.

I got up at the same time as Artie and followed him down the hall. We took the stairs to the second floor, and he pointed to the left. We passed by two doors before Artie opened the third and stepped aside politely to allow me to enter first. It was a typical bedroom with cream-colored furniture. The nightstands were antique-looking and made of white painted wood.

Artie pointed to the left nightstand. "That one's mine."

I nodded and walked over, pulling out the drawer slowly with my gloved hand. I looked down to see...

A gun.

A gun and a box of bullets.

I looked up at Artie, keeping my face as blank as possible.

He stepped forward and leaned over.

His eyes widened.

Artie looked shocked as I pulled the gun out and set it on the bed.

I knew little about guns—being mostly bulletproof thanks to my uniform, I didn't much care—but it looked like an antique police officer's issue revolver, silver in color. I could tell it had been recently fired. The smell of gunpowder was still strong enough to be detected in the air. "Is this yours?" I asked, pointing to the gun on the bed.

Artie shook his head. "I've never seen it before. I had a gun years ago, but I never owned one again." Now Arthur Dallas looked frightened. "That's not mine."

When I saw the paper, I was about to close the drawer and then open the one on the other side to check it. It was folded in such a way that it was most likely placed there in hopes it would not be noticed for a while.

"Do you know what this is?" I asked him, holding it up.

"No." Artie shook his head slowly. "No, I've never seen that before."

"Do you mind if I look at it?" I asked him.

Emma's rules percolated in my mind the moment I laid eyes on the gun. Now, Artie had led me to the gun, so I was reasonably confident I was on solid legal ground for having discovered it, even had it been used in the commission of a crime.

I wasn't so sure I could read the folded paper without permission, and I didn't know what it was evidence of—if anything.

"I don't know," Artie said, then he shook his head. "Jody is in and out of lucid thinking, and...I just don't know." Artie's expression was pained. "I don't know what's going on here or why that gun is in my drawer, but I think..." He trailed off and gave me a helpless look. "Am I under arrest?" He swallowed. "Or is Jody?"

I'm not one to just look at the nearest obviously crazy person and think murderer. Most people with mental illnesses were good people who struggled with brains that didn't quite do what they needed to do. They weren't bad people, and they weren't necessarily aggressive people.

But...dear old Dad had a point.

Artie knew Jody better than I did, and he clearly knew that his son had his issues. His question indicated that Jody might be unstable and perhaps a danger to himself or others—but he'd said very little that was specific.

I had to admit, though—Jody seemed out of control. His barfing up the location of the possible murder weapon also seemed too…convenient.

I looked at Artie, then down to the gun, then back up at him.

I didn't want to jump to conclusions. I needed to discover who owned the gun first before I accused anyone of anything. I needed to know when it was fired. Whose fingerprints were on it.

Oh, yeah—and if it was the murder weapon.

I knew none of those things for sure.

But at the same time, I wasn't so naive that I could ignore the warning bells going off in my head. It probably was the murder weapon. This family was probably connected somehow. This paper in my hand was probably evidence of something.

I sighed and set the paper down without reading it.

I needed to call Emma.

"I'm going to call a detective to the scene, Artie," I told him. "And I need you to go downstairs, get your wife off her call, and not come in this room. Not even up to this floor. Okay? Will you do that?"

I tried to smile at him and make it all look routine.

"Artie!" his wife called up the stairs.

I pulled the door open and motioned for Artie to go downstairs. He smiled at me sadly and entered the hallway. "I'll be down in a second, honey," he called to Millie.

"Hurry up!" she shouted. "I want some lemonade!"

Artie sighed and turned to face me. "You think it'll be my gun, somehow, don't you? I never thought it would happen to us. I had no idea Jody even owned a gun." He shook his head, looking down at the floor. "Astra, I'm a good person. I work hard, I do the right thing. I always try to do the right thing. But…"

"But what?" I asked softly.

Artie looked up at me. "He's my son. I love him. I can't just throw him out. He's been in and out of trouble, and I thought…I thought I could handle it. I thought I could make him do the right thing. I can't…You know, I was just about to…" The confident man crumbled in front of me, anguish palpable around him.

"It's okay, Artie," I said. "We'll figure it out."

"Thank you, Astra." He gave me a sad smile and disappeared down the stairs.

I pulled out my phone and called Emma.

"Yo," she answered quickly. "What'cha got?"

"Possibly the murder weapon," I told her and explained what I'd found.

CHAPTER TWELVE

*D*etective Emma Sullivan arrived with the cavalry.

Granted, the cavalry appeared to be barely out of high school—and, to be honest, some probably were—but they did an excellent job of fanning out across Arthur Dallas's home.

Emma, who appeared older and more confident than her breathlessly youthful crew, seemed to have a good grasp of the situation from the moment she walked in. She calmly pointed in various directions, giving each officer orders before sidling up to me. "Thanks for calling me." She frowned as I rolled my eyes. "No, I really mean it. Now, if you would just call off your stupid owl down at the station, my day would improve several times over."

"I told you I would. This gun could clear Jason. My owl will leave the station as soon as Jason does, and you know it," I deadpanned, smiling as best I could. "Anything else?"

"I know," she replied but then shrugged. "I had to ask. Jason's mother came to the station, by the way. She knew exactly who Archie was, and I think you may have earned quite a few girlfriend points for sending him."

Jason Bishop's mother, Lillian Thornton, served as the mayor of Forkbridge's more-psychic-than-thou sister town, Cassandra. While Forkbridge's paranormal-leaning citizens consisted of just my family (the witches) and a club owned by Emma's brother (a vampire), Cassandra had spiritualists and ghosts in almost every house in their weird enclave. Jason's mother was the top spiritualist as well as Cassandra's mayor—and my police captain's girlfriend.

"How's Captain Harmon doing?" I asked Emma. "Ms. Thornton must be furious at him."

"No, her fury is definitely reserved for me," Emma said, grimacing. "She wants the full story of how the arresting officer on her son's case"—

Emma hitched a thumb toward herself—"could be so stupid as to not realize he was completely innocent. I'll tell you all about it later, though. First things first: What did you find?"

"Upstairs." I pointed toward the staircase. "In the main bedroom."

"Let's go," she said, and she and I climbed the stairs together. I pointed at the gun and bullets on the bed when we entered the room.

Emma pulled on a pair of nitrile gloves and picked up the gun. She sniffed the barrel, placed it back down, and then lifted a bullet out of the box. Then, squinting at it, she asked, "Did you read either of these with your powers?" she asked, referencing my psychometry. "Even though you're, you know, not a cop, and you shouldn't be picking up things like guns and bullets with your bare hands at a possible crime scene?"

"Oh, ye of little faith. No, I didn't. I haven't touched either of those without my gloves on. This isn't my first time at the rodeo."

"This *is* your first time at the murder rodeo," Emma countered. She weighed the bullet in her palm, then turned it over and looked at the tip. "I know you've done stuff like this before in your 'other' life," she admitted, referencing my thirteen year paranormal military career, "but if I get any new evidence because of you, I may not be able to use it because of your involvement. We need it for court. It's different here in human land. There's no authoritarian witch council to execute people."

"You sound almost envious," I joked.

She glared at me. "The US military doesn't look kindly at talk like that. Watch it."

I held up my hands. "I'm the one who found the gun. I'm the one who found a suspect. I'm the one who called you for help. So get off my back, snippy. You should be able to use anything I found." I frowned. "Speaking of suspects, how I found that gun doesn't make any sense."

"It doesn't?" Emma asked, and she looked interested. "What do you mean?"

"I first heard Arthur Dallas's name from Gaston Priestpoint. I didn't ask him for it or anything, really, that could even lead to it. He mentioned the name spontaneously." I leaned against the dresser. "He just assumed, for some reason, Arthur Dallas was the person you arrested for Liberty's murder. Not Jason."

"Right, you told me that."

"Then when I came here, Jody Dallas, Arthur's crazy son, told me—also spontaneously—that there was a gun up here in his father's nightstand.

Maybe I just have a face that makes people want to spit out critical information to me," I said, although I didn't believe it. "I have to admit, though, both of those spontaneous statements seem...suspicious."

"Not to mention the fact that when I checked on Arthur Dallas downstairs, he didn't act like a guilty man," Emma admitted, her brow furrowed. "He acted like a man who had been falsely accused. He was falling all over himself to be helpful. Like he trusted me to unravel all this and was giving me as much information as possible."

"I had the same experience. He seemed shocked that there was a gun in his drawer. But, Emma, I'm telling you. Something's not adding up." I looked at the gun again, wishing I could grab it and read it, but I knew Emma would sooner tackle me to the ground than let me handle evidence bare-handed.

"Hinky," Emma murmured and looked down at the gun. Then, after a few moments, she looked back up at me. "Look, I am not oblivious to these suspicious synchronicities. And I do know your fingers are practically twitching to read that thing."

"A little."

"I can't let you do it. You're Jason's girlfriend, Astra, if—"

"Stop telling me things I already know. We're wasting time."

Emma nodded. "Okay. We'll investigate this a bit more before you risk completely ruining your chances of ever officially working with me again." She frowned. "We can figure this out."

Emma called a few forensic techs into the bedroom to process the scene. "I need everything dusted for fingerprints, especially that nightstand," she told them.

The techs busied themselves with that task as Emma walked into the hallway and called Captain Harmon.

I followed a few steps behind her and busied myself by looking at the photos on the hallway wall while she related what I'd found to the captain.

I looked up at a photo of two boys, one slightly older than the other. The younger boy had the same round face and dark eyes as Jody, but his dark hair had a reddish tint, unlike Jody's jet-black hair. The two held up trophies for some competition. I could barely see the names etched on the old—

Wait a minute.

"Emma," I whispered and pointed to the photo. "Is that Jody and Gaston?"

Emma kept the phone in her ear, looked at the picture, and then looked at me. "Well, they did grow up next door to each other, so that would make sense…" Her voice trailed off. "Forkbridge is a small town. Just because they knew each other as children doesn't mean they're still in touch. Necessarily." She sounded like she was trying to convince herself of something she felt in her bones was probably true. "No, Captain, I was talking to Astra." Pause. "Yes, sir. I know, sir."

"I need to check on something, and then I'll be right back," I told her. Since Emma was not the boss of me at this very moment, I took off to check the other bedrooms, leaving Emma on the phone with Captain Harmon.

* * *

Despite Jody Dallas being an adult, his bedroom appeared stuck in time. An unmade twin bed was pushed against the room's far wall beneath a Pink Floyd poster. On the other walls, faded posters of Tool, the Rolling Stones, and Led Zeppelin hung. A poster-board sign on his desk read OCCUPY FORKBRIDGE in big red letters, with a slew of "We Deserve Better!" quotes scrawled underneath. His desk was piled high with clutter: books, dirty dishes, and a cracked-open computer.

I shivered, and not because I was cold.

This room was filled with magic. I could sense it. It hummed in the air as if hundreds of invisible bees buzzed around me. It wasn't the magic of an old spell or a simple blessing or homeopathic cure like Althea might perform. When I reached out to touch a poster on the wall, a red spark leaped angrily from it to my finger. I could hear a faint snarl as it did.

This wasn't just magic.

It was dark, angry, resentful magic.

I took a book from his desk and flipped through it. Some pages had folded corners, indicating that he had read them several times. I took a quick glance at the first chapter, titled "How to Make Your Own Human Body the Material for Your Spells."

Jody Dallas wasn't mentally ill.

The man was in way, way over his head.

I was shoving the book back into place on the desk when I heard Emma's footsteps behind me. "Don't come in here," I said as I turned away. "Everything in this room is pulsing with dark, defensive, angry magic. You're human, I'm not sure what—"

"Oh, please." Emma walked dismissively in as if she hadn't a care in the world.

I cursed under my breath.

"Emma, this room could have an impact on you—" I was about to say something when Emma walked up and snatched the book off the desk. "What are you doing? I'm telling you, this room is—"

"I have no doubt that you and your magical star power, as well as your considerable paranormal military background, will be able to get me before permanent brain damage," she said, looking down at the book. Emma sat down on the edge of Jody's bed and leafed through it. "I don't know what all this is, but just the pictures look pretty dark," she said as she paused on a page. "Obeah talisman..." she muttered. "A gris-gris..."

"Can you not read random magic words out loud in this room, please?" I told her sternly. Humans. They could watch a hundred horror movies that began with some idiot saying words out loud that they didn't understand, and they would still do it when they had the chance, believing they were immune. "I don't even know what's in here yet, and you have no idea what you're saying."

"Yeah, right, sorry," Emma said. She flipped through the book then glanced up to the various bones, statues, and geometric images displayed on the shelves above his desk. "Jody Dallas is really into this stuff, isn't he? Is this Voodoo?" She glanced around the room, then back at me. "Can you really learn stuff like this from a book or a YouTube video?"

"No, but there's an awful lot of magical items running around since the Ministry shut down," I told her, glancing around the room. "Maybe he got his hands on something that fast-forwarded his progress."

Emma looked at me, then back around the room. "Do you think he's the one who magicked Unity's chest?"

"I don't know." I walked across the room, pressing my hand against the wall. The walls were emitting a strong, but not entirely unpleasant, buzz. I couldn't identify the pulsing magic against my exposed skin, but I sensed the power it was emitting. "I should go get Ayla. Maybe Aunt Gertie has a better guess at what's going on in here. The dead can see more than we can sometimes."

Emma nodded. She reached over and slid the old book back into place on the top shelf. "Yeah, go get her and come right back." Her fingers hovered in front of the other books. "I'm going to stay here and poke around."

I glared at her.

She glanced back at me and then rolled her eyes, pulling back her hand. "I meant I'll be waiting here, not touching anything. Obviously."

* * *

AYLA WAITED IN THE KITCHEN—JUST as I'd asked her to.

I explained what was going on as briefly as I could given that the officers were only a few feet away with Arthur Dallas and his wife. Then I lowered my voice and whispered, "It feels like magic is in the walls. But it's not a ward. It's just weird."

Ayla nodded as if that wasn't too surprising. "Aunt Gertie was in that room. She said she knows what's going on." Ayla opened her mouth a few times, then closed it as if she was trying to figure out how to say something. She glanced down the hallway toward the dining room. "I don't think we'll be able to talk privately here, though."

"We probably won't," I agreed. "Let's go upstairs."

Once back in Jody's buzzy magic bedroom, Ayla gazed toward a corner silently.

"Does she know what all this is?" I asked.

"She said she's pretty sure," Ayla said. "She wants to check it out again to be absolutely sure before we jump to any conclusions." Ayla put her hand on the wall. "I can feel it, but I don't think it's that strong. It's not that charged; it's like it's just...crowded."

"What's crowded?" Emma asked. "That's a strange word to use for a wall."

"I was answering Aunt Gertie," Ayla told Emma without looking at her. "Give us a minute, could you?"

I half-smiled.

Ayla's tone wasn't a request.

After a few moments, my sister nodded again. "Okay, Aunt Gertie's sure she knows what this is."

Emma held out her hand. "Don't leave us in suspense."

"She said there's a type of spell that does what's going on here," Ayla began and then paused. She nodded and then said, "It's called a spirit trap. It traps a spirit, doesn't kill it or make it disappear or anything, just keeps it in place, then releases it when you want it to. So people can use it for power."

I'd heard of it.

Nasty stuff.

"So there are spirits bound to objects in this room?" I asked her.

She nodded. "According to Aunt Gertie, it's a spell, like a summoning spell, but instead of calling a spirit from its place to the physical world, it just calls the spirit here and binds it to whatever Jody picks." Ayla frowned. "Some of them are just bound to this room because when he started doing it, he didn't do it right."

"So this room is a prison for angry spirits?" Emma asked her.

Ayla nodded. "Aunt Gertie's sure of it."

"Great," I muttered.

Suddenly, a burst of magic exploded from the chest against the wall, sending a shower of sparks across the room.

"Oh, and they'd like our help getting free, please," Ayla added.

The chest clunked.

"How in the world can we help?" Emma asked

me. "What do you know about spell-binding and summonings and things?"

I glanced at Ayla and shrugged. "Nothing. I mean, I know *about* them. But I was in the military. So any spells I learned were...um..." I looked uncomfortable at that and then said, "I guess you could say I was a little more focused on weapons."

"I'm not sure how much help I am," Ayla added. "I don't know that I can translocate a ghost out of the room and, anyway, the whole thing is a trap." My sister's head swiveled on her shoulders sharply. "Oh, really?" A pause. "Yeah, I can tell her." Ayla turned to me. "Aunt Gertie says your star magic should be able to fix it. The ghosts were unfairly captured." Another pause. "Just let it loose, and it should free everyone and take down the spells."

"Nothing works like that, Ayla," I told her. "There's no miraculous magic that just fixes anything it comes across."

"Aunt Gertie says your power does if what it's fixing is unjust."

"Ayla, there are a billion things that can go wrong with just letting loose some magical energy undirected." I cocked my head to one side.

"That's not going to work, and it would be crazy to even try that."

"Aunt Gertie says you're wrong because you don't have a magical power," Ayla said, schooling me like she was dozens of years older instead of younger. "You have a goddess power. You have the justice power. And until you trust it, you're not going to do anything with it." My sister turned to the corner and smirked. "You know, Aunt Gertie, she actually hasn't done anything— yeah, sorry, I'll tell her." Ayla blushed slightly. "Anyway, Aunt Gertie says if you can trust the power and let it go, the power will act on its own, and that's going to make it work."

"This is insane," I told her, but Ayla didn't budge.

She shrugged. "Do you want to help them?"

"Yes, but—"

"Then you need to trust the power," she told me, cutting me off. "You need to let it loose." Ayla turned toward the corner again and continued a conversation with my dead aunt in the room, which, in turn, included the invisible spirits detained all around us. "I know; she just doesn't have any confidence in herself," Ayla said, nodding in agreement.

"I swear, there are days I wish I'd never gotten out of bed," I muttered.

I stood there listening to one end of the involved and judgmental conversation, looking around the room and feeling the magical vibe emanating from every object. Ayla seemed confident in her—or Aunt Gertie's—explanation, and even though I couldn't see the trapped ghosts in the room, I could sense them.

I walked over to the object that had thrown sparks into the air and focused my attention on it. It was a simple wooden chest with nothing special about it, but it was almost crackling with energy. I ran my hand across the front of the chest, and my fingers tingled with yearning as I drew them away.

"All right." I took a slow look around the room. The atmosphere was tense, and every time I made eye contact with the chest, the poster, or the sword on the wall, it felt like they were all glaring at me, accusing me of failing to help them.

Though that might have been my imagination.

Another nod from Ayla. "Aunt Gertie says good. Remember. It's the justice power," Ayla told me. "It's the power you need to trust, to let go of your fears, and—"

"Stop lecturing me, Ayla, and get out of this

room. You and Emma." I glanced back at where Ayla was standing. "Now. Before I change my mind."

Emma looked at me for a moment, then grabbed Ayla's hand. Together, they left the room.

"I can't believe I'm doing this," I muttered to myself, though I'm not sure giving voice or thought to my reluctance made much of a difference. I had no idea how this would go or where to begin, but I knew I needed to be alone. I wasn't sure I could trust myself not to screw everything up, and I didn't want to electrocute my sister or Emma in the process.

I took a deep breath, then closed my eyes.

I called on the power to come unfurl around me, to use me to right the wrongs in this room. To come out and do what needed to be done.

And it did.

A massive, pulsing ball of energy erupted around me. It felt like an enormous fireball. Perhaps it was a circle of divine energy, pulsing and writhing against my skin like searching fingers. It wasn't painful or dangerous, but it was highly demanding.

A demand for freedom and justice.

"All right," I whispered to myself. "All right, let's do this."

It felt like a living, breathing thing. It tingled against my skin, the power of the goddess. And it felt...urgently alive. I could have sworn I heard it calling me, whispering begging me to let it go, begging me to let it loose. Demanding I allow it to set things right.

I took a deep breath and then said, "I trust you."

For a moment, my concentration broke, and I wasn't sure why I said that or who I trusted. Was it Athena, Astraea? The star magic itself? Ayla, Aunt Gertie?

Me?

I stopped my mind from racing and refocused.

Opening my eyes, I looked at the chest against the wall directly in front of me, took a deep breath, and released the power, sending it out all around me in a vast arc that suddenly became a wave.

The wave slammed into the chest, and the wood cracked in half.

Oops.

It shimmered through the entire room like a vortex and spread out.

I could feel it touching the ceiling and walls, outside the room and into the hall, and through the doors and into the rest of the house. I could feel my power connecting to every piece of wood in the structure, every stick, stone, and cement block. The energy was touching everything in every direction, every single object.

Then, with a satisfied angelic hum, it shimmered again brightly and disappeared.

Just like that.

All the power was just…gone.

No, not gone.

It was back within me.

I looked around.

The room seemed to be the same as it ever was. Nothing obvious had changed.

The posters were still on the walls, the sword still hung, the chest was still cracked in half. There was no glorious light show or magical energy, no electricity or fire or anything exciting. It was just a man-child's bedroom in need of a cleaning.

But…

The room felt lighter. No buzzing energy, no oppressive fury. It was as if a spring breeze had blown through. The room felt refreshed, less angry. Less dark.

And I felt…relieved.

When I turned around, the door was open,

revealing Emma and Ayla standing in the hall, unsure of whether to come in.

"Well?" Emma asked.

"I don't know," I told them, still in shock. "I did something."

The detective's eyebrow raised. "Did that something work?"

"It worked," Ayla said, her voice relieved and grateful. "Aunt Gertie says the spirits are very grateful to you for what you did. They were afraid they would never leave that room again." She turned to Emma. "She's bringing them back to our house so you can talk to them through Mom and me if you have questions." Ayla glanced back toward the room. "They wanted out of this place."

"I bet," Emma said, nodding.

"Do you still feel the magic?" Ayla questioned. "Do you feel the anger in the room?"

"No," I told them. "No, the room just feels lighter. It's...calmer."

"What do you think that means for Jody?" Emma asked, her eyebrow raised.

CHAPTER THIRTEEN

*E*mma led me down the stairs and into the living room where Arthur and Millie Dallas sat stiffly beside each other on a barge-sized sagging faux-leather couch. Mrs. Dallas glared daggers at her husband, her expression angry, while his eyes were fixed on the coffee table. A young officer stood over them, shifting on his feet.

"I heard something break up there," Millie told Emma coldly. "If you or you or you"—her long, manicured finger (sporting a *gigantic* emerald ring that flashed in the light) jabbed toward Emma then me, then Ayla—"broke anything in this house, I will call my lawyer and sue this rinky-dink department for everything it has and then some."

"You'll call a lawyer," I murmured and tilted my head. "Let me guess. You're represented by Wynn Rogers?" The gruff lawyer seemed to show up in every corner of this case.

So why not here, too?

Millie's face blanched as if I had kicked her in the stomach. Her mouth dropped open, but no sound came out

Huh.

Honestly wasn't expecting that to be a bullseye.

"No, ma'am," Arthur responded politely. "Our family attorney is Ruben Rudzik. He's representing us in a lawsuit handled on the other side by Wynn Rogers, though, so we're familiar with Mr. Rogers, aren't we, honey?" He turned toward his wife and smiled wearily, but she didn't meet his gaze. "But we wouldn't call him. No."

"There's no need to bring him up," she snapped. Her left hand moved to her throat, and she looked away.

"Who?" Arthur Dallas asked, looking confused.

"Lawyers," she snapped.

Emma and I quickly glanced at each other.

Millie Dallas had been the one to bring up lawyers. Not us.

And despite that, she still hadn't called one.

Emma sat diagonally across from the couch in an armchair that swiveled so she could face them evenly without towering over them. Ayla sat on the love seat across from them, and I stood just behind my younger sister.

I mean, a *little* towering intimidation wasn't always a bad thing.

"Have you had any recent contact with Wynn Rogers, Mr. Dallas?" Emma asked.

"No, ma'am," Arthur answered, shaking his head. "The lawsuit is at a bit of a standstill. Why?"

Millie's eyes shifted toward her husband. Her tone was icy when she spoke, the phrases tinged with a hint of venom. "Because they're trying to pin a murder on you, Arthur, and obviously, if you had, they would have something on you." She reached forward for a glass of wine on the coffee table. "Honestly, you're such an idiot. I'm shocked you're not in handcuffs already."

I watched Millie Dallas as she belittled her husband. Her words were full of contempt and disgust, and her body language spoke of years of condescension and cruelty. His shoulders dropped, defeated, and his eyes refused to meet hers. Finally, he looked up and smiled briefly at me.

If someone had bet me which one of the two people in front of me had shot a woman in the head, my money would have been on Millie without a second thought.

"Oh, Millie, I don't think there's anything like that going on here," he disagreed evenly. "This woman is a police officer." He gestured toward Emma. "She took an oath to protect and serve. There's no way she'd do anything illegal or unethical. She's not going to pin a murder charge on anyone. She's too professional for that."

"She's too professional for that?" Millie's eyes grew impossibly wide as if she was shocked. "What's wrong with you, Arthur? Did you hit your head? I swear, you're such a moron," she told her husband once again.

"Well, I'm sorry you feel that way," he responded patiently. "But I don't know anything about it, and surely they'll realize that after some investigation. The detective is just doing her job." Arthur smiled at Emma. "I understand."

Millie's eyelashes fluttered. "I'm sure they're desperate to pin it on you, Arthur. I mean, you're the most likely suspect, anyway."

"Why is everybody tangentially connected to

this case so ready to spit out Arthur's name as a suspect?" I thought, only I used my outside voice and actually said what I was thinking aloud. All heads turned to look at me. "Sorry, but that's three times today—Gaston Priestpoint first, then your son, and now your wife," I said, looking at Mr. Dallas. "All pointing fingers or assuming you're guilty."

Millie Dallas let out a disgusted grunt and downed half of the glass of wine in one swallow. "They found a gun in my husband's nightstand, you idiot. Obviously, he's a suspect."

"Or you are," I told her. "Or your son is. Or someone else that's been in this house but wants your husband blamed for the murder." Millie blinked. "We haven't pulled prints off that gun yet, so let's not get ahead of ourselves."

"My son? Me?" she gasped. "All right, I've indulged this ridiculousness long enough," Millie told me coldly. "I think it's time you and your friends left my home before I call the police to have you removed."

"You. Call the police?" I looked at the uniformed police officer. "Have *you* hit your head?" Officer Redgrave looked back at me, a perplexed expression on his face.

"Ma'am, we have a search warrant for this

house," Emma told the woman and pulled it out of her jacket pocket. She then slid the document across the coffee table to her. As Millie read it, she turned white and then red. "And we're going to be going through it thoroughly. We'll leave when we're done."

Millie Dallas stared at the document in disgust for a long time. Her icy gaze then shifted to her husband. "And I'm sure you'll find something to pin a murder on Arthur," Millie responded angrily. "You're desperate, and you're grasping at straws, but I don't care. I don't know anything about the murder, and I don't *want* to know anything about it."

Arthur's eyes widened, and he gulped.

"This is harassment, pure and simple," she added and tossed the warrant back toward Emma with attitude.

"You're welcome to call Ruben Rudzik or Wynn Rogers if you'd like, but we're well within our rights to conduct a search of your house. While my teams are doing that, I'd like to ask you more questions, if you don't mind." Emma's voice was firm but polite.

Millie laughed. "What questions do you have for me?"

"Were you familiar with Wynn Rogers?"

"I met him once or twice," Millie's cheeks turned slightly red. "In passing."

"Oh, no, dear, we met him more than that," Arthur said amiably. "Don't you remember? He handled the lawsuit Unity filed about our tree. We met the man dozens of times. Maybe even more than that. He also handled that problem Gaston and Jody had when they were in New York."

"Which problem was that?" Emma asked casually.

"You really are an idiot, Arthur," Millie snapped at him.

* * *

"Which problem did Wynn Rogers help with?" I asked Arthur again.

"Gaston and Jody?" I nodded to Arthur's question. "They were accused of stealing a sculpture from a gallery in New York City."

Millie laughed derisively. "It was not a sculpture. It was a rock. They probably picked it up in Central Park."

"No, Millie, it was a sculpture. I saw it," Arthur argued. He looked at Emma. "It was called the Muon." I raised my head. "It had an X carved into it, and it was a shiny black. No one knew who the artist was, but every sunrise and sunset, it would glow purple. The gallery said it was worth thousands."

"It was worth the two thousand and five hundred dollars they took as compensation and not a penny more," Millie corrected her husband. "But it wasn't a sculpture. It was just a rock." Millie glared at Emma. "Overzealous police officers weren't going to put my baby in jail because a rock fell in his pocket while he was visiting a gallery."

Fell in his pocket.

Wow.

"Fine, dear, it was a rock," Arthur Dallas agreed with Millie. "The gallery's owners were certain it was stolen from them and were quite certain Gaston or Jody took it. They said they wouldn't press charges if we returned it or paid for it, so we paid for it."

"You mean if they paid for it," I corrected.

Arthur Dallas looked at me quizzically.

"Gaston and Jody are both adults. Unless this happened years ago when they were children, whatever mistakes they made? It wasn't really your responsibility to fix them. Surely you made *them* pay for the rock."

"No, no, Millie was concerned that they didn't have the money, and they told us it was all a misunderstanding," Arthur Dallas said. "Gaston and Jody both swore it wasn't them. They said they were with each other the whole time, and no one had any time alone in the gallery to have taken it." He looked from me to Emma. "You see? They each vouched for the other. So we believed them. What else could we do?" He shrugged. "Unity wanted to let Gaston get arrested, teach the boys a lesson, but we"—Arthur's eyes flicked to Millie and back—"paid for the rock."

"I'm sorry, I'm confused," Emma said, leaning forward. "If they didn't steal the rock and it was, in fact, stolen and not returned, how did you two see it?"

Arthur and Millie looked at one another.

"It turned up," Millie told Emma shortly.

"And it was returned to the gallery owners?" Emma asked.

Millie gave Emma an odd look. "It was paid for by then."

"So you *didn't* return it?"

Millie rolled her eyes. "The gallery had all these ridiculous rules about where you could and couldn't touch the pieces. It was all part of the experience, they said." She laughed. "It was a rock.

You could pick it up and put it down anywhere! Who cares! I've had jewelry worth more money than that stupid thing."

"I'm surprised the gallery didn't sue you," I mentioned.

Millie laughed. "They did, but Wynn made sure they took the money and left the boys alone."

There it was again. "You mean Ruben Rudzik."

Millie frowned. "What?"

"You said Wynn made sure they left the boys alone, but Ruben Rudzik is your lawyer. Correct?" I leaned against the love seat. "You barely know Wynn Rogers, you said."

Millie Dallas's perfect posture wilted, and I swear I could hear her teeth grinding as she tried to figure out how to explain what she just said. Her thin nostrils flared with every breath she drew. Finally, after a few moments, Millie Dallas sat tall again and lifted her chin imperially.

"Maybe we should call our lawyer," Millie responded and then downed the other half-glass of wine. "I think we're done with your questions now."

"I'm not sure I have any more, so we'll leave the team here to finish up," Emma said, then pulled a card out of her pocket and handed it to the woman. "But if you're lying to me, I'm going to know, and it'll only make me more interested in knowing why. It's always better to come clean early."

"I don't know anything about Unity's murder, and I don't know anybody who does," Millie told her, then looked over at her husband. "Do you, Artie?"

"No, I don't know anything about Unity's murder, and I don't know anybody who does," Arthur Dallas said, mimicking his wife's statement word for word—though his tone was much more gentle. "I do hope you find out. I know she and I had our neighborly disagreements in the past, but she was a very nice woman."

"She was a greedy socialite viper and terrible to poor Gaston," his wife said. Millie raised her eyebrows at Arthur, and he shook his head with a sigh.

Emma stood.

"Show yourself out," Millie told Emma as she poured another glass of wine.

* * *

"WELL, THAT WAS..." Emma paused as she pulled the front door closed behind her.

"Interesting?" I offered.

"Utterly," she replied. "Ayla?" She looked over at my sister.

"Yes, Emma?"

"Who the heck is Aunt Gertie? Is she an honest to goodness ghost or some imaginary friend you've made up?"

"That is a long story," I said to Emma as we strolled down the driveway to our cars. "The *Reader's Digest* version is Aunt Gertie is the third Arden sister of the generation one up from ours. She died in a tragic tree branch accident that may or may not have had something to do with a love spell, and my mother banished her from our family's senses." Emma blinked. "She's been possessing Ayla for a few months trying to communicate with us to break the spell or... something, I don't know."

Ayla nodded. "Spell's broken now. I can tell you the story another time, Emma. But Aunt Gertie is kind of my spirit guide now."

I raised my eyebrow.

"What?" Ayla asked.

Emma waved me off. "Wait a second. You were possessed, and now she's your spirit guide?"

Ayla rolled her eyes. "You say that like it's a big deal. This isn't my first possession." Ayla paused in the middle of the driveway as Emma reached her car first and opened the door to get in. Ayla grew annoyed at Emma's dubious expression. "What? *Your* brother was hitching a ride to spy on you, and you two still hang."

"Ouch, Ayla," Emma told her in a hurt voice.

"Don't worry about me. I can channel ghosts just fine. Mom just didn't want me to."

"Right. Your head practically turned around on your shoulders for several months, and you were maybe a step or two away from spewing pea soup, but you can channel ghosts just fine," I said sarcastically.

"You're just jealous I know how to use *my* gifts," Ayla muttered.

"Hey, now—"

"Right. Okay," Emma said, cutting me off. "Before this turns into a catfight, let's drop it for now. We'll discuss this another time." She shook her head. "Or never, because I don't think I'm ever going to feel entirely up to speed about all this stuff even if you explain it again." Emma opened the driver's side door to her car, sat down, and closed it. She paused and looked at me through the open window. "I don't know where I'm going. Where am I going?"

"To the jail to release Jason?" I offered.

Emma glared. "Nice try."

"If you're going to work with me on this, I think we should head back to Arden House," I told her, gazing down the road toward my home. "Althea's been digging around on the internet, so she may have new information, and I think we need to go somewhere we can talk openly about the magical aspects of this case."

"The rock?"

I nodded. "And the chest. Among other things."

Like Wynn Roberts's name continually popping up, the ghosts locked in a room.

You know, the usual stuff.

"Okay, I'm going to put a BOLO out for Jody Dallas. I didn't get to question him, and I need to after what happened in that room. Let's hope there's a good explanation for this." Emma started her car. "And let's hope he tells us. I only have so many jail cells available."

"You'll have one more if you let Jason out."

"Yep. And nope." Emma tapped her fingers impatiently on the steering wheel of her car. "Let's go. Daylight's wasting. If Jason didn't do it, I'd like to let him out before Valentine's Day."

"You can do that any time, you know," I retorted, then got into the Jeep and pulled away from the curb. Emma turned on her blinker and turned right at the end of the Dallases' driveway to follow me.

"She wants to let him out, you know," Ayla said, glancing in the rearview mirror.

"Who?"

"Emma." Ayla paused. "She's nice, you know. I know she's snarky and can be a little blunt, and it's not fair she's so pretty, but she's nice."

"Yes, she is."

"She wants to let Jason out, but she can't, you know."

I swallowed. "I do know. She's just doing her job."

"It sucks."

"Yes, it does." I looked over at my sister and smiled. "We'll figure it out."

Ayla nodded back with a serious look on her face. "Damn straight, we will," she responded in a tone that was deeper than her usual tone.

CHAPTER FOURTEEN

$\mathcal{B}$y the time we all got settled into the living room to discuss what we'd discovered, Mom and Aunt Gwennie were already arguing with an empty space in the air. They sat imperiously on their favorite old couch (patched so often that a quilt would have wanted to date it). "I don't care how many ghosts were anchored to one room, Gertrude, it simply could not have been done without multiple people doing the spell casting. It's not possible!"

"Or one of the Ministry's magical cheating items," Aunt Gwennie added, nodding. She gently took a rose from a bouquet on the end table and handed it to my mother. "Here, Minerva, try and stay calm, dear."

Mom's nostrils flared as she gave Aunt Gwennie side-eye.

My aunt's normal air of quiet deference to my mother, the high priestess, had gone right out the window since Aunt Gertie had shown up. I wasn't sure what changed the dynamic between the two women and whether it would be permanent—but it was entertaining.

"I don't need one of your *calm down* roses, Gwen."

"Oh, I really think you do," Aunt Gwennie disagreed.

Ami looked at me with one eyebrow up.

"Good grief," I muttered.

"Did you say something, Astra?" my mother's voice snapped at me like a whip.

"Nope." I sat up and leaned forward toward Emma. "Do you want to start with what Aunt Gwennie has to say about the ghosts, go over what we discovered in the interviews, or find out what Althea knows after an afternoon of internet sleuthing?"

"Might I suggest we start with the internet sleuthing?" Althea piped up, taking a seat cross-legged on the floor in front of the knotty pine coffee table. "I already know what the ghosts said, and it wasn't much." She plugged a projector into her laptop and turned the beam toward the white wall. "Okay, can everybody see?"

We all murmured that we could.

"I concentrated on a few people," Althea began, hitting a key and displaying a neatly symmetrical table of people with images. "Unity, her maid Allegra, and her children Liberty and Gaston. I added Arthur and Jody Dallas, and Wynn Rogers later. And then, finally, I added Millie Dallas because—well, here." She hit a few keys, and a photo taken from Instagram popped up, replacing the suspect wall.

There, projected five feet tall, was an image of Millie Dallas dancing with Wynn Rogers. He was dressed in a tuxedo. She was dressed in a tight-fitting black gown that hugged her form and flared out below her hips like a crinoline. Their heads were tilted toward one another, and their eyes locked.

"Barely knows the guy, huh?" Emma murmured, surprised.

"Wait, it gets better," Althea said and hit a key. And again. And again. At every significant social function the two attended, they managed to be photographed together dancing.

Or sitting beside one another at a corner table.

Or whispering to each other in a back hall.

"I got these photos from the back end of a photographer's website. You know, the password-protected area they use so people can buy photographs?"

"How'd you get the password?" Emma asked her.

"Well, I found this one on Millie's Instagram," she told Emma, clicking until a photo of Millie, alone, appeared on the screen. "See the photographer's stamp at the bottom?" Emma nodded. "He recycles his passwords—or, more specifically, he gives everyone one of five passwords. A quick search turned up all five, and from there, it was just a matter of going to Millie's directory on this site and trying all five."

"You ever thought about going into law enforcement?" Emma asked, her tone impressed. "The way you went about this? I think I can use this if those passwords are public."

Althea gave a faint laugh. "No, thanks. I like my potions."

"Why would she lie about knowing Wynn Rogers?" I asked, frowning. "And Arthur Dallas is missing from all these pictures as if he wasn't even there. If that's the case, not only did Millie lie about the times she met the lawyer with her husband, it looks to me that she lied about meetings hubby may not even know about."

"Maybe she knew Wynn planned on killing Unity," Althea answered and tapped her keyboard again. "These were filed in the courthouse this afternoon. Unity left half of her estate to her two kids equally. There's no trustee for that half, so nothing weird there. But the other half of the estate? That's where it gets interesting."

Unity's will created a charitable trust managed by Rogers Investments, Inc.

"I don't get it," Ayla said, frowning. "What's a charitable trust?"

"A charitable trust is a form of irrevocable trust, which means you can't cancel it or make any changes once you create it," Emma said slowly. Her eyes scanned the document on the wall intently. "Unity is saying that she wants half of her money put into a trust that will donate to charities of her choice as well as support the people she names as beneficiaries." She squinted. "And one of the beneficiaries of that trust is Gaston Priestpoint."

"So it pays her kid and donates money?" Ayla asked. "That's weird."

"Rich people do lots of weird things," Emma agreed.

"Wait. Gaston gets money from it, but not her daughter, Liberty?" Aunt Gwennie asked.

"No," Althea said. "I told you, that's where it got weird. And this is a charitable *remainder* trust, which means the beneficiaries get a set amount every year, and whatever's left over is donated. They'll get a hundred thousand dollars every year for the next fifty years. So they're set for life. And Gaston isn't the only beneficiary."

"He's not? Who else?" I asked.

Althea paused dramatically and then said, "Jody Dallas."

Emma and I looked at each other.

"I know I never met the woman, but I find it hard to believe she would cut her own daughter out of the trust. Not to mention the situation with Allegra Ochoa," I told Emma. "She was paying for the maid's medical treatments and had done so for a few years. There's no way she would just cut her off like that. Unless this is an old will?" I looked at Althea.

"The will was signed less than two months ago," Althea said, scrolling down. "And it was drawn up by—"

"Let me guess. Wynn Rogers," I said.

* * *

"Is that legal?" I asked Emma. "Wynn Rogers acting as the executor on a will for a trust that he'll ultimately manage? Well, I assume he'll ultimately manage it."

"Legal? Probably. Ethical?" She shrugged. "Maybe the bar association will have something to say about it. I have no idea." Emma tapped her finger against her knee. "Technically, he didn't inherit anything, though. He executed a will, and he's—I assume, too—the owner of Rogers Investments. Technically, he didn't benefit."

I rolled my eyes. "No, he just has control of a multi-million dollar trust."

We all sat quietly, staring at what the entire room seemed sure was the reason Unity Priestpoint ended up dead.

And yet I felt like we were missing something.

Emma glanced over at me. "What?"

"In the grand scheme of things, this would be life-changing money for these people," I said as I pushed up and walked toward the projection. "In this situation, I'm not sure it is. Did Unity hoard her gold like a dragon? Refuse to give her kids any help? I mean, why kill her now?" I scanned the names. "Which one of these people couldn't wait?"

"Everything pivots on Wynn Rogers," Emma

said, pointing. "But no, I get what you're saying. The murderer could be Wynn, Gaston, Liberty, Jody. Any one of them had a motive. It could be an agreement between all of them. Or two of them."

"Millie," I added.

Emma tilted her head. "Is Millie a beneficiary, too?"

"No," I answered. "She's just mean."

The detective chuckled. "Fair point."

"So, do we go talk to Gaston? Liberty?" I asked. "What do you want to—"

"Wait." Emma held up her hand. "I want to know what the magic stuff is that's at play here. While I appreciate your help with the ins and outs of the case, this woman was found in a chest that had magical symbols all over it." Emma looked around the room. "Why?"

"We have a theory on that," Aunt Gwennie said and urged us toward a table at the end of the room. A small chest no bigger than a jewelry box sat in the center. "We recreated the chest you found, though it's much smaller. The symbols on it are exactly the same. Minnie?"

Mom nodded and grabbed a crystal art piece off the shelf. She held the small square mosaic. "Astra, do you remember where this came from?"

"Sure, Ami made that when she was younger," I said, gesturing toward my sister. "I think she made it for you for Mother's Day when she was young. Right?"

"Right." Mom leaned over and placed the mosaic in the chest. Then she closed it, put her hand lightly on the top, and waited a few seconds. Finally, with a nod to Aunt Gwennie, she opened the chest and pulled out the art. Then, holding it out to me, she said, "Take off your glove and read that."

I raised my eyebrow but did as I was told.

Images flooded my mind. Only the memories of the art piece weren't toddler Ami gluing shards of crystal onto a butterfly. It was Jason Momoa, dressed in tight jean shorts and nothing else, making bedroom eyes at me as he affixed crystal to the frame.

My eyes flew open. "How did you do that?"

"This chest is ensorcelled specifically to counter and confound a power like yours," Aunt Gwennie explained. "There's no spell. It's all done through the interaction between the symbols and the wood."

"Oh, I'm totally taking that when we're done with this investigation," Ayla breathed excitedly. "You all heard me. I called dibs."

"That means someone knew you could read her body and find out who killed her," Emma said with a gleam in her eye. "And what you saw was what that someone wanted you to see. Not what happened."

"Explains why I saw her shot somewhere she couldn't have been."

"A tall man with dark hair and a black robe," Emma murmured. "It's almost like they were trying to tie up everything neatly with a bow. The magical chest, the murder, everything."

"But not too tidy," I pointed out. "I never saw his face."

"What about my butterfly?" Ayla asked. "We know Unity is at Liberty's house. So that probably means Liberty was the one that shot her, right? I mean, it has to be. If she has her mother captured in an object, there's probably a reason for that."

"Out of every possible suspect we have, Ayla, Liberty Priestpoint seems the least likely suspect. Yes, her call for the well check seems odd. Yes, she'll inherit money from her mother's will. But it's Gaston connected to Jody, and Jody who wound up running a prison for wayward, trusting ghosts in his teenage bedroom."

Emma nodded. "I have to agree with Astra. There's little pointing to her."

Ayla frowned. "But we also haven't talked to her very long, either."

"Oh?" Aunt Gwennie asked.

"Gaston was over at her house doing the mansplain thing. Only he didn't explain anything and wouldn't let her talk, either," Ayla said with an eye roll. "Honestly, I hope he did it. He was kind of a jerk."

"Are we convinced Jason didn't kill Unity, then?" I asked Emma.

The detective nodded. "Pretty much. None of the evidence we're uncovering points to him."

Finally.

"Awesome. Let's go let him out."

"You bet," Emma told me. "Just as soon as we find someone else to put in the cell instead."

I glared at Emma angrily. "You just *said* you don't think he did it."

"True. I did just say that. But as long as he's in jail, whoever did kill Unity thinks I think he did it." She held up her hands. "Besides, you have your owl guarding him. No one's going to come near him. So he'll be fine."

Emma had a point, and as much as it

frustrated me, I knew she was right. "You're a horrible person."

"Other people seem to think so." Emma looked over at me. "We can't let anyone get away with murder, and this helps a little. Besides, if we gave Jason a choice whether to help us out, what do you think he would do?"

I glared back and said nothing.

"Astra, I need a little more evidence than a butterfly and a chest and a will, and you know it. We have, what, four suspects? Five if you count Liberty? And the gun is still being processed."

"Six with Millie. Look, I am not about to let anyone get away with murder," I said, giving her my best steely glare. "Ugh. Fine." I pointed. "Let's make a murder board."

* * *

I STARTED to leave the room to grab a whiteboard, but Althea waved my effort away, tapped a few keys, and brought up the six suspects.

Gaston Priestpoint.
Liberty Priestpoint.
Jody Dallas.
Millie Dallas.
Arthur Dallas.

Wynn Rogers.

"That's really not six people," Ami said, looking at the list. "Well, I mean, it is, but it's more than that. That's two families and a lawyer."

"Two families that lived next door to one another," Mom added.

"And sued each other," Althea said, pulling up a list of lawsuits between the two neighbors. "A tree sat on both of their properties, and Unity wanted it to stay up. Millie wanted it down. They fought like cats and dogs over that stupid tree. Five lawsuits over twenty years."

"Millie said something when we were leaving —that Unity was a greedy socialite viper and was terrible to Gaston," I told Althea. "You have any idea what she was talking about?"

Althea nodded and tapped a few keys. "Gaston didn't make a whole lot of money. It's pretty clear Unity wasn't helping her kids out as adults at all. In fact, it seems to me from Gaston's financials that after the theft in New York a couple of years ago, Unity cut him off entirely." Layered over the murder board was Gaston's credit report. Two years ago, his substantial number of credit cards went into default practically overnight.

"My vote is for Gaston," Aunt Gwennie said. "Can you imagine what it would feel like to have

244 | LEANNE LEEDS

your mother hand over a bunch of money to the maid but cut you off without a penny to your name?"

"We don't usually decide this kind of stuff by vote, but I appreciate your input, ma'am," Emma said with a smile. "Your family has definitely been some help on this case."

"Can we go back to Millie and Wynn?" I asked. "I know what she said when we were at her house, and she was emphatic that the family didn't know him that well. Arthur wasn't in on the subterfuge, and Millie practically laid into him for mentioning they'd met a few times during the various lawsuits." I pointed toward the projection. "Those pictures weren't taken in court."

"So they knew each other at Forkbridge social events," Althea said with a shrug. "Do you really think that's suspicious?"

"It is when three separate people in two places, all of whom are on that list, all pointed toward Arthur Dallas as the murderer," Emma told Thea. "And honestly, if Artie wasn't such a wet noodle with sociopathic-presenting family members, I might take a closer look at him. A gun *was* found in his bedroom, in his nightstand."

"That his crazy kid told us about," I pointed

out. "The kid that's buddies with Gaston. Who mentioned Arthur as a suspect in the first place, if you'll recall."

"But Gaston directed us to Wynn Rogers, and Wynn said he doesn't represent them."

"Aunt Gertie says—" Ayla tried to break in, but I talked over her.

"That's technically true, but he's running that trust fund," I told her, pointing. "Maybe he's not technically their lawyer, but he's not unconnected to them. He didn't mention that. You don't find that suspicious?"

"Hey," Ayla tried again. "Aunt Gertie says—"

"I find all of it suspicious," Emma responded, also talking over Ayla.

"Hey! I'm trying to talk here!" Ayla shouted. "Can you people shut up for just thirty seconds so I can get this out?"

We all stared at her.

"Sorry, but you need to learn to listen," Ayla grumbled, shifting beneath our stares. "Aunt Gertie wants you to know that she's been hanging around Forkbridge for years, and she knows a lot of gossip no one else does. Some of it she's seen with her own eyes. One piece of gossip is that Millie"—Ayla pointed—"and Wynn? They've been having an affair."

"Are you sure?" Emma asked.

"I'm not, but Aunt Gertie is." Ayla held up a finger, looked toward the empty corner, waited, and then nodded. "They've been meeting once a week at the Four Corners hotel in downtown Forkbridge. Millie claims it's a once a week work drinks thing, but it's not."

I hated conspiracies.

And this was looking like a conspiracy.

"You shouldn't be peeping on people, Gertrude," Mom told the empty corner. Seconds later, her eyes grew wide. "That's all I'm saying. People need their privacy." Pause. "Yes, I know you're a ghost. You can still have respect for people's—"

"Did Mom just lecture someone about *privacy*?" Ami asked me, shocked.

My mother's indignation was swift. "Do you have something to say to me, Amethyst Arden?"

Ami tried to suppress a smile before meeting her gaze. "No, ma'am."

"I think it's time for us to visit Liberty's again. Maybe we'll get lucky and Gaston will still be there." Emma looked at me. "They may not have talked to you, but I have a badge. They'll talk to me." She looked down at Ayla. "What's the deal with the butterfly?" Ayla explained what the butterfly was doing and its behavior when we visited earlier. "Okay, then you'll come, too."

"You don't want to go back over to the Dallases' house?" I asked, surprised. "The police are probably still there."

"Exactly," she nodded. "The police are still there. Do you know where they aren't? Liberty Priestpoint's. If Gaston is there, we can question them both. If he's not, there's a good chance he ran off to meet Jody Dallas, and it will give us a chance to question Liberty Priestpoint without her brother's interference."

"Okay, sounds like a plan," I agreed.

Looking down at Ayla, Emma added, "You and your aunt can take this opportunity to find Unity Priestpoint. If she's in that house, I'd like to talk to her—and if someone trapped her with that stolen magic rock thing, we need to get her out."

I blinked. "We didn't even talk about the magic rock and the ghosts. How'd you put together she might be trapped?"

"Detective, remember?" Emma patted herself on the shoulder. "You know, before you showed up, I sometimes figured things out all by myself."

CHAPTER FIFTEEN

"So talk to me about this rock. Is it one of those fancy military things that walked out of your armory after the paranormal world coup?" Emma asked as we made our way to Liberty Priestpoint's home for the second time that day. "If it was, how did it wind up in New York City for an art exhibit?"

"I don't know, and I don't know," I said from the passenger seat of Emma's old—but finely tuned and super fast—Chevy Malibu. The engine growled and purred, almost like a jungle cat. "The Dallases called it the Muon. A muon's a subatomic particle, if I'm not mistaken."

"You think it's like the ghost trap from *Ghostbusters*?" Emma asked.

I waited for her to continue, but she didn't. "The what from where now?"

Emma gunned the engine. "The ghost trap from *Ghostbusters*. It's a movie? Really popular movie, too. From when we were kids." She glanced at me. "Didn't you people watch movies growing up?"

"We watched movies," I told her a little defensively. "Occasionally."

"It's this movie about these scientists that go out and take care of ghosts in New York City. Like an exterminator? But for hauntings." She moved her hand from the steering wheel to the gearshift and then back to the steering wheel. "Anyway, I don't know if they explained it in the movie, but I played the video game. I am sure they called it a muon trap in the game."

"Aunt Gertie says muons are elementary particles that were discovered in cosmic rays. They have no charge, they are unstable, and they are heavier than other similar-sized particles," Ayla called from the backseat. "When a muon comes into contact with an atom, it can cause that atom to decay, which is what happens to the atoms of a ghost when it is captured by the ghost trap."

I turned and stared. "The ghost trap? Are we

talking about the movie or the rock? Does Aunt Gertie know something we don't?"

"She says that would be the understatement of the year," Ayla responded glibly.

"Wait a minute. If I remember right, muons exist for only two microseconds before they decay into other subatomic particles," Emma said as the interior of her Chevy Malibu turned into a science class for which I clearly hadn't taken the needed pre-requisites. "They can't do anything or be used for anything because they barely exist."

"Says the human driving her car with two witches, a ghost, and a Greek goddess's star energy locked up in my sister's gut like a bad burrito delivered by a snarky owl working for UberImmortals delivery. Tell me more about things that don't exist," Ayla quipped with an eye roll. "Look, maybe the muon rock that got stolen isn't about the actual particles. You said *Ghostbusters* was an old movie—"

"I did not," Emma shot back.

"From when you two were kids?" Ayla responded snarkily. "That's old."

Emma looked offended. "Watch it, whippersnapper."

The detective did not, thankfully, see Ayla's youthful eye-roll.

"Anyway, my point was maybe it just took the name from their ghost trap. The thing from the movie. You know, because it does the same thing?"

That made much more sense.

Or, more to the point, I understood that concept, at least.

Millisecond-existing elementary particles?

Like I didn't have enough things to figure out at the moment.

I turned to the back. "Ayla, did Aunt Gertie talk to any of the ghosts we released from Jody Dallas's room?" Ayla nodded. "Did she get any information?"

"Basically, they were all just passing by too close to the house, and WHAM! They got sucked into the place like they were caught in a tractor beam." Ayla's hands went toward her head and mimicked a big suction cup on her skull. Then she jerked forward as if yanked by some unseen force. "They didn't notice what was going on until they were caught, and by then? They couldn't leave. There was a shoving match with some other ghosts that had been in the room a while because some of them wound up in objects that other ghosts were already in."

"But after he caught them? He didn't do anything with them?" Emma asked her.

"Not that they said, not after that, no."

"So not helpful." I sighed, returning my gaze to the passing scenery outside the car's windows. "Just more confusion." I blinked and turned. "Unless Jody wasn't capturing them for any specific reason." I looked at Emma. "Maybe they were just practice."

"You think he was just capturing random ghosts to learn how to use the Muon?"

"That makes sense," Ayla said. "They said they weren't able to be heard or break out or whatever." She paused, looked to the empty space next to her, and then nodded. "A few knew they couldn't break free on their own, that they had to be released. But no one ever actually was released, so maybe…" Ayla held her hands up.

"Maybe he could capture them, but he doesn't know how to release them," I guessed. "And that's why his room was crowded with ghosts like chickens in a cluster."

"All begging to be let out?" Emma asked, glancing at Ayla in the rearview mirror. She nodded. "Maybe that's what drove him off the deep end. Having to sleep in a room where a bunch of angry souls are shouting at him?"

"But he couldn't hear it," Ayla said.

"Just because he couldn't consciously hear it doesn't mean his subconscious wasn't processing all that energy being thrown at him from all those ghosts." I turned. "How many ghosts were in that room? That buzzy energy I felt seemed to indicate a lot."

Ayla looked at the empty seat next to her. "Really?" she asked, shocked. "Aunt Gertie says there were well over a hundred. It was overstuffed with angry spirits. Like an extra cheese pizza pocket. But with ghosts."

"See? That'll drive you nuts," Emma murmured.

"You didn't meet the guy. He seemed nuts."

Emma pulled into Liberty Priestpoint's driveway, and I pushed my worries about the Muon away. Let's face it—it probably was a stolen military weapon from Imperatorial City, it probably had been used exactly as we thought, and it probably was in Liberty Priestpoint's house somewhere if Ayla's butterfly actually worked.

All I could do was get it back and get whatever ghosts had been captured out of it.

* * *

LIBERTY PRIESTPOINT OPENED THE DOOR, but only halfway. She looked frightened. "What do you want?"

"Liberty, I'm Detective Emma Sullivan," Emma said, stepping closer to the half-open door. "We spoke on the phone a few hours ago?"

"I know who you are. I don't want to talk to you."

Liberty tried to close the door, but Emma's foot shot out to block it from closing. Anger flashed across Liberty's face.

"Ma'am, we—"

"How dare you? You don't have any right! Get your foot out of my door!"

"I could get the right with one phone call, ma'am, but I'd prefer not to do that unless absolutely necessary." Emma's expression was stern but not hostile. "We're not going anywhere until you talk to us. We have questions about your mother and your brother we need answered."

Liberty's face softened. "My mother?" she asked. "What about my mother?"

What on earth did she think we were here to talk about?

"Could we come in?" I asked.

Liberty was barefoot; her skin was white like

milk glowing in the dim light of the hall. Her hair was in disarray, and her eyes were bloodshot as she stood in her knee-length white nightgown. "I don't think this is a good idea," Liberty said. "I don't feel well, and Wynn said I shouldn't talk to the police without a lawyer."

"If you'd like to call him, that's your right, ma'am," Emma said. "I'd be happy to wait for him to arrive if you'd like. But we do need to talk to you."

Liberty hesitated, then pulled the door open and stepped back.

"Is there anyone else in the house?" Emma asked, glancing toward Ayla. My sister gave a barely perceptible shake of her head. "Your brother, perhaps? Or your husband? Your children?"

"My husband's in Europe on business," Liberty told Emma as she led us into the neatly decorated living room. A blue afghan was draped over the back of a sofa. An old-fashioned coffee table in front of the couch held a lamp and a ceramic ashtray with a half-smoked cigarette in it. A newspaper was folded on the coffee table, its face-up headline reading: LOCAL TEACHER SHOT DEAD. "He's trying to get a flight back. The children will be here tomorrow."

Emma, Ayla, and I sat on the sofa while Liberty took one of the armchairs.

Liberty leaned forward and set her elbows on her knees. "I'm really not feeling well," she repeated, sounding worn out and terribly sad. "What's this about my mother? What questions do you have?"

"I appreciate your willingness to sit down with us. I know this must have been a hard day for you. First, I'd really like to know why you didn't just go by your mother's house to check on her." Emma pulled out her notepad and a pen. "It just seems odd to me that you would call for a well check instead of calling your mother yourself or calling Allegra to check on her. Her phone was working, and her home is just a few miles away."

Liberty's expression creased, and she appeared to blink back tears. "Mom and I got into a fight a couple of months ago." Liberty shook her head and looked away. "It wasn't a nice fight. We...we said bad things to each other. Hurtful things. But honestly, that happened a lot."

Liberty reached toward her coffee table and picked up a pack of cigarettes. She shook one out, and Emma looked at me, then to Ayla, who gave a slight shrug.

Liberty lit up, took one puff, and then stubbed it out.

"What was this most recent fight about?" I asked.

"Same as it always is, I guess. Our personalities clash. That would be a good way to put it." She took a deep breath and let it out slowly. "She was angry at me for a long time after I got married. She loves—loved her grandchildren, don't get me wrong, but she disliked my husband for some reason. And she felt I was...well, let's just say I never lived up to my potential."

"That happens between a lot of parents and children," I said quietly.

Liberty leaned back in her seat and rubbed her eyes. She was crying. "She was just so angry, and it didn't matter what I did; she always found something else to be critical about. She would tell me to my face how terrible I was, how I didn't know how to do anything right. Yet her maid, Allegra?" she added bitterly. "Allegra could do no wrong. All of the students she rescued? No wrong. But me? I was always wrong."

We'd heard no story that even hinted at such a tense relationship between Liberty and her mother, Unity. Still, Liberty's expression was marked by deep anguish. This could be nothing more than a suspect coming up with a hook and a line, but if it was, wouldn't she want to downplay the animosity?

"I'm sorry," Emma said simply. "So that's why you called the police instead?"

She nodded. "She's still my mother. After Gaston told me about his meeting with her, I was worried."

Emma and I glanced at one another. "What meeting?" I asked her.

"My mother is—was a very opinionated old woman." Liberty gave us a tired smile as she caught herself speaking about Unity in the present tense. In the following sentence, though, the present tense was back. "She doesn't think I speak up for myself enough. She's always giving me advice about managing my children and my husband. She's never approved of my husband to begin with, even though he's a wonderful man." She bit her lip. "I'm sorry. I think I told you that already."

Emma nodded. "That's all right. Take your time."

"The fight was about me," Liberty said, her voice thickening. "Gaston told me that mother told him she was going to cut my children and

260 | LEANNE LEEDS

me out of her will." She laughed harshly. "It wasn't surprising, really; she's been threatening to do it for years. I told him not to worry about it."

"You did? Why?"

"Like I said, my husband is a good provider. My children are already off on their own." She shrugged. "I don't need some crazy inheritance to be happy. Pierre's money never made my mother happy. But I think it was the hurt she intended to cause that…" Her voice trailed off, and she wiped away tears. "Anyway, she'd been telling Gaston for months that she was going to cut him off, too."

I frowned.

According to Gaston's financials, Unity Priestpoint cut her son off two years ago. Not two months ago. I looked at Emma and raised an eyebrow.

"When did this argument take place again? The one with you and your mother?" Emma asked.

"About two months ago," Liberty answered. "It was just before Christmas. Mom and I haven't spoken in all that time." She looked hurt, almost as though she couldn't understand it herself. "I only found out about the will because the lawyer called me." She shook her head, looking lost. "That's when I called Gaston, then Gaston went and confronted mother, and he confirmed it." Liberty wrapped her arms around herself and stared at the coffee table, her expression distorted by grief. "And now we'll all never be able to forgive each other."

So, the young Priestpoints only discovered their mother was cutting them out of the will because of a phone call from Wynn Rogers.

Two months ago.

"Liberty, we've seen the papers. The will was filed with probate court today," I told her, leaning forward. "You're still in the will. You and Gaston split half of your mother's money and assets. The other half goes into a trust."

Unity Priestpoint's daughter looked confused. "No, I'm sure you must be mistaken."

"No, Astra's not mistaken," Emma told her. "The will was signed two months ago. You were —are—still in the will."

Liberty looked at us with silent disbelief. She shook her head. "But Wynn Rogers called to tell me I was cut out of it." She frowned and got up. "I'm sure of it. I think I even still have the voice mail he left for me to call him." Liberty picked up her cell phone off a side table, tapped the screen, and Wynn Rogers gruff voice filled the silent room.

"Liberty, I wanted to call and let you know that your mother has decided to redo her will. I'm not sure what the situation is between you kids and Unity, but she's decided to cut you both out of any inheritance," he said. His tone was slightly angry. "I'm going to try and talk to her, but I wanted to give you a heads up that she's on one of her vindictive warpaths. So maybe avoid visiting for a bit, give me a chance to try and work on the situation. Call me. Bye."

"And I did," Liberty told us, tapping her phone. "We—my mother and me—did speak a couple more times, but it just degraded into a fight. Well, degraded into her yelling at me."

"When did Wynn Rogers leave you that voice mail?" I asked.

Liberty said the date and time.

"Three days before the new will was signed," Emma murmured.

This all started with Wynn. Everything traced back to him.

"Do you mind if we look around the house?" Emma asked. "We'll be careful; we won't disrupt anything."

"Yes, of course. I have nothing to hide."

She might be the only one.

Emma nodded at Ayla and me, and we rose from the sofa.

* * *

WE TOOK LESS than five minutes to find black rocks arranged in a circle on a knickknack table upstairs. A larger black rock was in the middle of the ring—with an X crudely etched in the center.

Ayla's blue butterfly flapped up at us excitedly.

"Well, I bet I can guess what that thing is." Emma pulled out her phone and snapped pictures. Then, pausing, she dropped her phone to her side. "Why am I doing this? I can't include that thing in evidence."

I tugged off my glove. "I can read it."

"Let me get my butterfly first." My sister smiled at her butterfly and reached out to the larger rock in the center. "Come on, buddy. You did an awesome job."

The blue butterfly jumped on her hand, but Ayla's fingers brushed against the muon rock. She jerked back a step as if she'd been shocked. The rock flew into her palm—seemingly of its own accord—and glowed.

I stepped back, my stomach twisting at the

sudden change, and hastily pulled my glove back on. It was not a soft, gentle glow. Instead, it was a blinding white light, and the room hummed with energy.

Suddenly, the rock in Ayla's hand gave off a high-pitched squeal that made me wince.

"Ayla!"

"I'm not doing it!" she gasped.

Ayla leaped back, almost as though she'd been physically pushed. The rock fell to the ground, and the stone's light flickered, growing dimmer and dimmer.

"Ayla?"

The light from the rock finally faded completely. I exhaled in relief and bent down to pick it up. I didn't touch the stone with bare hands, though.

"I'm fine," she told me. "I don't know why it reacted to me. Sometimes my butterfly—" Suddenly, Ayla paused and stared at an empty space in the room. "Are you Unity Priestpoint?" Another pause. "Oh, wow, yeah, no problem. Though I don't know what I did."

"We should find out where Liberty got— Emma? Emma, what are you doing?" Detective Emma Sullivan was crouched, gun drawn, pointing her pistol toward the rock. "What on earth were you planning on doing with a gun?"

"I wasn't going to just stand there and let something attack us." She shot me a sharp look as she holstered her weapon once again. "You have magic. I have bullets."

As she finished her sentence, the door to the bedroom burst open, and Jody Dallas came careening into the room, yelling gibberish I couldn't understand. His hands were outstretched, and he was moving so fast he didn't seem to notice anyone else in the room. Jody's eyes were wild and unfocused.

The blue butterfly fluttered around the intruder's head like it was trying to attack.

"Freeze!" Emma shouted, her stern voice stopping all movement. The audible click of the weapon's safety being removed seemed to hang in the air. All color drained from Jody Dallas's face. "See?" she said to me, not taking her eyes off Jody. "Guns. They're useful."

"It that whole face to real!" Jody shouted. "Please you that to! Need it! Need it to that, yes!"

As the three of us tried to comprehend what on earth the guy was saying, he collapsed to the ground and wept like a child.

CHAPTER SIXTEEN

"What the heck was that?" Emma asked, staring at the defeated Jody Dallas. He looked back at her with a crestfallen expression on his sweaty, red face. "I didn't understand a word he said."

"Don't look at me," I told her. "They were words, but I didn't understand what he was talking about."

Jody Dallas sniffed and wiped the tears from his face. Then, with a deep breath, he looked up and glared at me. "You that for and go out no five!" His face flushed with anger. "Five!"

Ayla looked at me, her eyes moving from my face to the face of Jody. Then her mouth dropped open. "Oh," she said quietly. Shocked and staring, her gaze traveled back to me. "Oh, wow!"

I glanced at her. "What?"

Ayla's eyes moved back to Jody's face, and then she squinted. "He has a lot of other people in his head. Like, crammed in there. His mind is like a bag of crayfish, with everyone desperately trying to find a way out."

"Five!" Jody hollered and then nodded. "Five that to for save tinker!"

Ayla snorted. "Dude, you've got more than five people crammed into your head. With just the people stuck in your frontal lobe, you could populate a small town."

"Yes," Jody Dallas replied. "I'm. I'm!" His face turned crimson with anger. "Five!" His face showed his frustration as he stared up into each of ours. "What five that for two!" He burst into tears again when we didn't respond.

"Right." Emma's attention shifted between Jody and Ayla. "This is going to be embarrassing for me, I'm sure, but I'm going to ask anyway. What is he talking about, and what are you two talking about?"

"So, I think Astra was right." Ayla stepped slowly around Jody Dallas and leaned against the open bedroom door. "He had to practice using the rock to capture ghosts, and he wasn't very good at it at first. We know about the ones in his room in objects and such, but I believe he slammed a few into...well, him."

"What are you even doing here, dude?" I asked him.

Jody Dallas shut his eyes and sighed. "The boom. Boom. Five. Two and they five yell go." He slapped his hands against his head as if trying to swat a swarm of flies off his skull. "Five. Five and go nut tell stay."

I looked at Ayla and raised my eyebrow.

"So, my theory—and this is just that," Ayla aid, "is that your starlight explosion tracked him down in some way. You freed the ghosts stuck inside his room, but what about our bodies? They are biologically programmed to hold our souls in place. So, like, you opened the first jail, but not the second. They're still in there."

"Yes, yes!" Jody's face brightened. "That need it. Yes!"

"He's got all those ghosts he kidnapped running around inside him, tethered to him, struggling to speak through his mouth and use his brain. We're not built for it. He's...struggling."

Emma's eyebrows knitted together. "So, he's possessed?"

"Yes!" Jody nodded, then his face fell. "No."

"You aren't possessed," Ayla told him "You're...overloaded."

"Yes!" Jody pounded his fists against the floor in triumph. "Your help." Jody Dallas looked at me earnestly. "You. Help. We."

Emma let out an audible snort. "My finely honed cop gut is telling me *this* guy is likely the one that shot Unity Priestpoint. He lived next door. He had the rock. He had the magical knowledge to create the chest. So yeah, I think there are more people involved, but this guy is definitely involved. And he wants us to *help* him?"

"Just because he's talking doesn't mean that's Jody Dallas's words, Emma," Ayla told the detective. "He's got a bunch of people in there. Any one of them could be asking for help in getting out of the dude's head."

Jody's mouth snapped shut, and his head snapped up, his gaze focused on me. "Tell. Help. Out."

"Astra, I don't think you should do this," Emma told me. "I don't have to know what's going on to know that..." She trailed off and gestured at Jody. "Look, this could all be some ruse. People have been known to fake insanity to get out of a murder charge. It's not unheard of."

"Ayla!" Jody Dallas shouted, his anger momentarily flaring again. "Tell!"

"Yeah, he's not faking," my sister told Emma, her voice stern. "You can say a whole lot of stuff about this strange case, but one thing you can't say? This is fake. That dude isn't faking anything. I can see all the people stuck in his head." She leaned back. "Besides, it's not Astra that would do this."

"It's not?" I asked, surprised.

"Your power didn't free them," she pointed out. "If you could, it would be done already."

Well, little Ms. Ayla was gaining confidence at a pretty alarming rate.

"Help!" Jody Dallas repeated, his face tight with fear.

"Oh, for goodness sakes. Fine. So, what's the plan?" Emma asked, looking at Ayla. "How do we fix this?"

Jody took a deep breath and then nodded. "Yes. Fixed." When the detective continued to stare at him, he added, "The rock. It broke free. They're free. Zoom. Yes." Jody Dallas leaned back, his gaze unfocused. "Yes." He smiled as if his mind let go of the here and now and pulled him back into a happier time.

"So, what's the plan?" I glanced at Ayla, and

my sister shrugged, her expression thoughtful. "Do you not have a plan? Should we call—"

Suddenly, she held out her hand. "We've got it. Give me the rock."

"Wait a minute—"

"I am!" Jody Dallas shouted, his face twisted with a mix of agony and anger. "I help them! Help five!"

"Dude, be quiet," I hissed at the crazy man still planted on the floor. "Ayla, we know little about this rock or what it does. Are you sure that—"

"Either you trust me, or you don't trust me, Astra," Ayla said, her expression confident and her hand still outstretched, palm open. "We know what we're doing, and we'll get it done without harming anyone." Her expression turned wry. "I'd rather not mention that Aunt Gertie and I know a lot more about ghosts than you do about goddess starlights, and you didn't kill anyone when you detonated your psychic gut bomb. But, you know, I will if I have to." She raised one sardonic eyebrow.

Ayla's expression and speech remained those of a teen, but her demeanor, bearing, and confidence had changed massively since Aunt Gertie arrived. I looked into her eyes and saw no fear or nervousness. I might have believed her if she had been a soldier under my command.

She, on the other hand, was not a soldier.

She was my younger sister.

And the guy drooling at my feet was probably a murderer.

"Do you really want to try this, Ayla?" I asked her. "It's not easy to fix broken things. Broken people? That's way harder."

Ayla's gaze flicked to the insane man, then back to me. "I got this. I'm sure of it."

"Yes, fixed," Jody Dallas repeated. "Yes."

Ayla's hand remained extended and steady.

I gave her the rock.

She palmed it and held it out over Jody Dallas's head. She lifted her other hand, and I heard the words she said, but when I tried to recall them later, I found I couldn't. There was a flash of light that blinded me for a moment—like a stage light popping in the room. A soft whoosh filled my ears, like a low-flying jet, and then—

The rock disappeared into thin air.

"Oh, snap!" Jody said excitedly. "You're awesome!"

He was psyched for about thirty seconds.

Because that's how long it took for Detective Emma Sullivan to pull out her handcuffs and arrest Jody Dallas on the spot. "You've got the right to remain silent."

"Oh, snap," he said glumly as Emma led him downstairs.

* * *

"WHY IS HE IN HANDCUFFS?" Liberty asked, her expression confused. "He just stopped by because Gaston believed his speech problems were because of the stone he gave me." She turned and glanced toward the kitchen. "Isn't that right, Gaston?"

"Hey, bro, I'm good now!" Jody yelled, his head swiveling in the same direction as Liberty's. "These witches did something with, like, a tap on the head, and all the people in my head disappeared. Along with the rock, which is a bummer, but, you know, I can think again."

"They didn't disappear," Ayla told him, frowning. "They'd still like a word with you. You may want to say a few prayers before you go to sleep tonight."

"Yeah, no, that's fair, I guess," Jody acknowledged with a shrug. "The problem is these people think I shot your mom, man, and I'm in handcuffs. So, you know, that's kinda not cool, bruh. Can you come out here and tell them I was with you that night? Gaston? Dude, you in the bathroom, or what?"

I cast a glance at my sister, who had moved to the window and was standing with her back to me. Her posture gave the impression she and Aunt Gertie were in a huddle, talking, and I suspected they were discussing something they didn't want us to overhear.

Gaston poked his head out from behind the bathroom door. "I'm here, dude!" He stopped, blinking at the sight of the handcuffs. "Oh, snap! Why you in handcuffs?"

"Man, that door isn't that thick, dude," Jody told his bro with an annoyed look. "Don't you listen? I just told you."

"Naw, bruh, wasn't," Gaston told him with a shrug. "But we can deal with this right here, you know." Liberty's brother hitched his head toward the kitchen. "Wynn is here with me. He went to the kitchen to get some food."

"Wynn Rogers is here? In this house?" I asked.

"Yeah, man." Gaston's expression turned frosty. "Which is why you shouldn't have been in here asking my sister about Mom's murder. I told you when you were here before we got nothing to say. You arrested Jody's Dad—"

"Yeah, bruh, no, they didn't. That's what I was trying to tell you when my head was all wonky," Jody cut off Gaston and frowned. "They were at our house and stuff and they found a gun in my Dad's bedroom, but Dad's at home with Mom. Only one in the Dallas family going to jail is me." He turned and showed Gaston his handcuffed hands.

Emma let him turn slightly and watched the exchange intently.

"But someone was arrested," Gaston said, frowning.

"Jason Bishop, a local teacher," Liberty told him as she moved toward her coffee table. "I have the newspaper right here."

Ayla walked up to me and pulled out a pad. Then she wrote HE IS LISTENING FROM A ROOM AWAY on the paper and showed it to me. I raised my eyebrow. WYNN she scribbled.

"Bruh, my Dad told me that chest you had me work on for Wynn was at the crime scene. You know, where your mom was found?" Jody looked calm but slightly confused. "How did it get there?"

"What chest?" I asked innocently.

"I've been messing around with occult stuff for a

long time, you know? And I found a way to make a box that could clear evidence of any…um, evidence. I worked on this box for months, wrote some of the best spells I ever wrote on it, but I needed a massive piece of oak to make it work right." Jody shrugged. "Wynn offered to buy it from me, and I needed the cash. I don't, like, work, you know?"

"So it doesn't just clear the objects of psychometric memory. It wipes all evidence away that might point to a crime or the person that committed a crime?"

Jody's head swiveled as he glanced at everything in the room except where I stood. "Yeah, pretty impressive, right?"

"Useless for a civil litigator," Emma murmured, her hand still wrapped around Jody's arm. "Really useful for someone that wanted to commit a crime or defend criminals."

"Wait, stop with the box. No one cares about your stupid magic box," Gaston told Jody sharply. "Jason Bishop was arrested for killing my mother? Not Arthur Dallas?" Liberty made a little shushing noise and set her hand on her brother's shoulder. "No, Liberty, that doesn't make any sense."

I narrowed my eyes. "Because you wanted to

frame Arthur Dallas for the murder of your mother so no one would suspect you?" I asked.

Gaston looked stunned, his brows rising. "What? No! My mother may have been a hard woman to live with, and she may not have been the most supportive mother in the world, but she was my mother!" He looked at his sister. "Our mother! I would never have killed her! Are you kidding me? That's sick!"

"Who told you Arthur Dallas killed your mother?" Emma asked.

"Wynn."

"Me as well," Liberty added. "Wynn told me, I mean."

"And you?" I asked Jody. "You pointed to your father as a suspect as well. In fact, you more or less accused him of murder earlier today when we were at your house."

"I kind of remember something like that, and stuff, but that wasn't me," Jody responded, his face now concerned that the tangible evidence, aside from a few items here and there, appeared to possibly be tightening a noose around his neck. "You gotta understand, Wynn was paying me to figure things out with magic, you know? And the ghosts he had me capture?" Jody shuddered. "Man, I shoulda charged extra."

I blinked. "Hold up. He directed you on *who* he wanted captured?"

I thought about not asking the question.

I knew Wynn Rogers was in the house, listening, as his (probably) carefully constructed conspiracy fell apart amid the "bruh" and "bro" discussion. I'd walked into this room sure Jody had shot Unity, and I was no longer sure of that. Jody Dallas was quite lucid and eager to explain everything he'd done, now that he was free of ghostly inhabitants.

Which Wynn Rogers might not want him to do.

"Well, after I learned how to use the rock, yeah," Jody nodded, his tone eager to explain. "Wynn had this rock he bought from some guy in Dallas, right? It's got a lot of magic. Wynn's been collecting magic stuff like that over the years. He's always buying stuff on the black market, too, you know?"

I raised my eyebrow. No. We did not know.

I pulled out my phone and texted Ami. DO ME A FAVOR. PUT SOMETHING IN THE BOX, AND TELL THE BOX YOU WANT IT TO CREATE EVIDENCE THAT I MURDERED UNITY PRIESTPOINT.

There was a short delay. UM. WHAT??

JUST DO IT PLEASE.

Jody continued. "So I started doing jobs for Wynn, you know? Like I was a full-time employee. Almost. Well, sorta. He'd give me the magic rules, a few clues, and I'd solve the problem. He'd be excited like he couldn't believe I figured everything out so fast and what a good job I'd done." Jody winced. "I didn't get paid enough, really. But it was fun, I guess."

My phone vibrated. I PUT A PAPER IN THERE. WHEN IT OPENED BACK UP, IT WAS A PICTURE OF YOU AND UNITY FIGHTING.

Not definitive.

But not real, either.

"Where did you get the wood to create the chest?" I asked Jody.

"Wynn got it from—"

"Yeah, okay, okay," I said, turning toward Emma. "I don't think these guys had anything to do with this. I think this is all Wynn's doing." I listened for any reaction in the other part of the house but heard nothing. "Or maybe Wynn and Millie Dallas together." I looked around the room. "Have any of you been *in* that chest?"

They looked back at me as if I were crazy and shook their heads no.

"I can read them and see," I told Emma,

pulling off my gloves. "It's the only way we're going to be sure. Well, relatively sure. This is pretty convoluted, and that was before you added in magic rocks, magic boxes, and some dude from Dallas."

Emma paused and then nodded.

I lifted my hand, cracked my knuckles, and extended both hands toward Gaston and Liberty, one on each side. "If you could come over here, please?" They stepped forward and held out their hands. I grasped each hand and stood quietly for a while, sifting through their sibling memories. There was a faint buzzing in my head, but nothing I saw or felt screamed MURDERER.

"Okay," I said, dropping their hands. "Now you." I moved over to Jody, who flinched slightly. "Nervous, Mr. Dallas?"

"I'm handcuffed," he responded, his tone snarky. "So, yeah, a little."

Again, the buzzing. Again, the images.

Again, nothing about a murder or even discussions of one.

I shook my head. "I don't see anything." I turned in the direction Wynn was potentially hiding. "You're going to have to come out, Mr. Rogers. Time for me to check you."

He stepped out from the hallway, his hand

over his eyes, peering like a cat into a dimly lit room. "I know you know," he said, his voice defeated. "I can see it on your face. There's no point, I guess."

Most people don't realize approximately 80 percent of crimes are solved by confession. Guilt is a heavy thing for people to carry, and regular people that commit criminal acts often have trouble dealing with it. Hand them an excuse, back them into a corner, and they'll do the rest of your work for you.

"Whatever I know, I'd like to be sure," I told him with a nod.

Wynn Rogers stepped across the room and put his hands on mine. I felt my magic grow, spreading through his body to seep into his skin.

He winced.

"Are you trying to keep me out?" I asked.

"No," he answered glumly.

Almost immediately, I felt the current of his thoughts and the swirling of the dreams that haunted him, to the point where I got light-headed and had to let go. "He didn't kill her, either," I said as I put my gloves back on. "He arranged it. He put all the pieces together to make it happen. But he didn't think this is how it would end." I glanced at his face. "He didn't pull the trigger. But he knows who did."

"I don't! I don't," he protested and then broke down in tears. "I hate this place," Wynn Rogers said, the words muffled. "It's so dark. I can't get away from it. It never ends."

"It ends when you tell us what we need to know. Confession really is good for the soul, you know."

He shook his head. "I don't know! I didn't see it. I didn't see anything. I don't know anything for sure. I don't."

"Wynn, what are they talking about?" Liberty asked, her face frightened.

He just stared at her. His face didn't change. For a long moment he didn't say a word. "I'm so sorry, Liberty. This isn't how I wanted all this to end. I was angry at your mother, but I didn't want this to happen."

"What?" Gaston asked him, putting his arm around his sister. "Wynn, what are you talking about?"

Wynn Rogers sat down, his regret palpable, and told his story.

CHAPTER SEVENTEEN

*E*mma and I looked at each other as Wynn
Rogers finished.

"Well, that was a gigantic waste of time,"
Emma muttered, glaring at Wynn.

Wynn looked shocked. "But I told you
everything I know!"

"The problem? That's everything we knew,
too." I shrugged. "Well, mostly. You didn't
enlighten us about anything other than your
faking the theft of the rock to explain why you
were coming around Gaston and Jody all the
time."

"Thank the gods. I was afraid you'd think I did
it," he admitted, wiping sweat off his forehead. "I

mean, um, I assume you realize I didn't do it. From what I said."

The story was surprisingly devoid of specifics. Or sense.

Liberty watched me carefully. "Well, I didn't know any of this was going on." She turned toward Gaston. "How could you work with this man to manipulate our mother? It was just money, Gaston. Building chests to fake wills? Capturing mother's ghost?" Liberty's eyes teared up. "You didn't want what you thought was fair, Gaston. You wanted to punish her for not being the mother you wanted her to be." Liberty turned to Wynn. "And you, you were in this for nothing more than greed. I don't know that I ever should have trusted you."

"Liberty, I—" Wynn reached out toward Unity's daughter, but she turned away.

"Leave me alone."

"Okay, let's all take a deep breath here." I turned toward Wynn. "Everyone connected to this case kept mentioning Arthur Dallas as a suspect." I narrowed my eyes. "I don't have to tell you that your affair with Millie Dallas makes you look pretty suspicious." The lawyer had confirmed his multi-year affair with Millie Dallas during his meandering, self-explaining not-guilty-of-anything confessional. "Everyone also implied this lawsuit about the oak tree is still ongoing."

Wynn nodded. "It is."

"Let's not get sidetracked with a tree in a dense forest," Emma said, leaning forward. "Back to Arthur being a suspect. Was this just you planting the seed that he'd done it?"

Wynn shook his head. "Jody told me." He pointed.

"Yeah, man, naw, I don't think so." The Dallases' son sighed, his chest deflating. "Look, when I started grabbing the ghosts, I maybe wasn't sure how to anchor them in objects, right? So a few got stuck in my head. Rattling around. Not many, but a few. There was this one, though, that kept using me to talk. Just one. Like I didn't get 'em stuffed in a corner enough. It was one of the early ones. Maybe she talked, because I don't remember saying that," Jody insisted, folding his arms. "Nope. Not at all."

"How did you know how to do that?" I asked.

Jody shrugged. "I don't know, books?" Jody's arm shook as he jangled the handcuffs. "Let me go, and I'll show you."

"Not a chance," Ayla deadpanned and then turned to Wynn. "Why did you want him to learn to capture ghosts? What was the purpose of paying him to learn death magic?"

Wynn hesitated, then his shoulders slumped. "I don't know. It was just fun."

"Wait, how did you pay him?" Liberty asked.

"Through the law firm," Wynn answered quietly.

"Through my mother's accounts, you mean," Liberty spat back fiercely.

"Look, Millie was furious at Unity for keeping her family in Forkbridge!" The lawyer's eyes were wide. "Because of that stupid oak tree, neither house could sell, Millie couldn't move to Los Angeles with the company for her promotion, and she and that jerk of a husband couldn't divorce!" He turned and stared at Liberty. "I was the lawyer on the case! I should have been able to do something, but your mother was impossible! Our lives were all stuck because Unity wouldn't cut down that stupid tree!"

"So Millie asked you to give her son a job," I guessed.

"It was the least I could do! It's not like I could do anything else!"

"Yeah, Ma's a pistol," Jody Dallas said, nodding. Arthur and Millie Dallas's son seemed unaware of the possible inherent irony in his statement. "I wanted to do magic for a living, though. I mean, you do." He pointed at me. "Why shouldn't I?"

"He finally had a good direction in life," Wynn explained. "It was a positive development for him."

"No offense, but I don't think you're in a position to judge," Emma said irritably.

"Did you ever tell your mother that you were doing this ghost thing with Wynn?" I asked Jody.

"She thought it was a great idea. Of course, she did!" Wynn's face flushed as Jody responded excitedly. "She was always on about ghosts and how much she'd love to talk to Grammy again."

Millie Dallas had numerous reasons to be dissatisfied. She had a husband she no longer loved, a child who was more concerned with the occult than with finding a real job and an adult life, and a tree whose roots bound her to a city and a marriage—I assumed—she no longer desired as her own. Every time I mentally examined the stumbling blocks to her escape, all roads led back to Unity Priestpoint.

"Unity's will—did you use the chest or a ghost?" I asked Wynn.

"Oh, that was a ghost," Jody piped up cheerfully. "I used the rock to put the ghost in her, and then I told it I would let it out after Unity signed the will. Unity wouldn't even remember. I mean, yeah, okay, we had to make sure Liberty and Gaston were taken care of, and since I helped, my Mom insisted I get a little something-something for my trouble, too." He looked pleased with himself. "So Wynn added it in. And I know it looks bad, right? But—"

"You really don't know when to shut up, Jody," Wynn said, shaking his head.

"There's a ghost still hanging around behind him, hovering," Ayla said, gesturing toward Jody. "She's muttered a few choice words about how he's just like his idiot father, but that wasn't what caught my attention."

"Oh, yeah, that's my Grammy's ghost." Jody turned as if to look behind him, then shuddered. "I can't even look at that thing. Well, not that I can see her. But she's creepy. She was the one talking through me a lot, I think." He shrugged. "I don't remember anything she said, though."

"And Grammy is?"

"Millie's mother," Ayla told me. "She's been saying more than that. In fact, she's been going on about how everyone in this room is an idiot, and thank the afterlife her daughter took matters into her own hands." Ayla smiled at the thin air. "Yeah, lady, I can see you. If you'd bothered to pay attention, you'd have known that earlier."

* * *

EMMA CALLED FOR A PATROL CAR, and it took only a minute or two for Officer Diamond and his partner to show up at the scene. "Watch these people," she told him. "That one over there is detained but not arrested yet."

"Yes, ma'am," the young officer nodded.

Ayla, Emma, and I gathered on the porch.

"Millie Dallas?" Emma said. She tilted her head. "I mean, yeah, these people—some of them —committed fraud, and that lawyer should be disbarred about seven times over, but even Wynn Rogers seems a little shell shocked that someone actually shot his former client."

"So, long and short is: Unity is rich, Unity is mean, Unity is in the way. Wynn and Millie start exploiting Liberty's money as well as hatching a plan to get everyone some cash when she dies." I raised my eyebrow. "Is it really that simple?"

"It usually is," Emma pointed out.

"It explains why Jody Dallas was in Unity's will," Ayla pointed out. "It's Millie's kid. She wanted to make sure he was taken care of and had money in case her divorce from his father went sideways, maybe." We both glanced at her. "What? I started watching *Law & Order* with Althea."

"Which one?" Emma asked.

"Which one what?"

"Which *Law & Order*?"

Ayla's eyes widened. "There's more than one?"

Emma nodded, and then her face tensed with concentration. "So, we can go over to Millie's, try and get her to crack, but there's one issue we can't get around." She tapped on her phone and pulled up a report. Turning the screen, she held it up. "That gun has Arthur Dallas's fingerprints on it. Even if we arrest her, she'll never be convicted. I have one person in jail, and that was a mistake."

I glared at Emma. "You know, I told you s—"

"Shut up," Emma said, cutting me off. "I get it, and I don't want to hear it. If this gets prosecuted —and I'm not convinced it would—the defense can point to Jason, they can point to Arthur, and we can't explain any of this at all. We go in talking about kidnapped ghosts and evidence tampering magic chests, and we'll both lose our jobs."

"Then Millie needs to confess," I told Emma.

She frowned. "I bet she's going to be a tougher

nut to crack than these guys were. Ugh. I know you've helped me close a lot of small cases, but on the big cases, Astra? You and your magic crap are a real pain in the—"

"Hey!"

"This case isn't messed up because of Astra's magic," Ayla told Emma with a serious look. "This case is messed up because those people in there messed around with magic they didn't understand to try and fix a problem. Don't blame Astra. Without us, you might have sent Jason or Arthur to prison."

Emma stared at my younger sister with surprise...and then respect. "Okay. You're right. Fair point."

"Do we have anything other than circumstantial evidence against Millie?" I asked. "And do we know for sure none of those numbskulls in there participated in planning the murder? Wynn's story dovetailed way too neatly with what we already knew."

Emma paused and then shook her head no.

"So, if she won't confess, what do we do?"

Emma tensed and averted her gaze. Ayla and I exchanged a look. My sister wasn't always the family diplomat, but there was a steely determination in her gaze that made me realize that might be about to change.

"I think you're going to have to be the judge here, Astra," Ayla told me. She glanced at the patrol car and then back at us. "Shake her hand, zap her with that justice juice, and make her confess if she's guilty." My sister placed a hand on my arm. "After all, the goddess would have done far worse for far less, right?"

"Wait, you can do that?" Emma asked, her eyes alight with excitement.

I probably could.

But just because you can do something?

That doesn't mean you should.

* * *

ATHENA *WOULD* HAVE DONE FAR WORSE for far less.

I remembered a story about an Arkadian princess who was also Athena's priestess. She gave birth to her illegitimate son within the goddess's sacred enclosures, and as a punishment Athena cursed the land, forcing the king to exile the girl and sell her into slavery.

Athena struck the first king of Troy blind for removing the Palladium from her burning shrine. As if that wasn't enough, in retaliation for their king desecrating her temple she unleashed a plague on the people of Opuntian Loris.

I mean…yeah. Some crazy stuff in the myths. Athena may be a modern feminist icon, but that was an evolution from the vindictive, rampaging deity full of wrath for those that crossed her.

Then again, I didn't have Athena's energy within me. Astraea, the goddess whose magic I did have, was more indignant and disappointed with humans than particularly wrathful and murderous.

I was subdued on the way to Millie's. I didn't like how Ayla had suddenly become the ultimate authority on all things Astraea, and her information came from an aunt I'd never heard of until a few days ago. An aunt my mother claimed was a murderer.

Then again, who was I to judge?

I'd done things in my military career I wasn't proud of.

I missed Archie.

I appreciated his watching over Jason, but I felt a little naked without my raptor sidekick constantly giving me advice—at least a quarter of which wasn't bad, and at least three-fourths of which at least made me laugh.

"Are you going to do it?" Emma asked me.

"What?"

"Shake her hand and zap her with the justice juice."

I rolled my eyes. "Can we not call it justice juice?"

"A fairness zap? A due process dollop? Morality mangling?" Emma said, running through a variety of suggestions, each one worse than the last. "A pang of proper justice?"

"Those started out bad and are getting worse as you go."

Emma shrugged. "You got me. The point is, will you do it?"

"Yeah, I will. I guess. Maybe," I said noncommittally. "I'm not happy about it, but…"

"I didn't think you would be."

"Why not?" I asked.

"Astra, you're a nice person. You're a close friend who I care about, and you have a pretty high standard when it comes to justice, right and wrong. Despite the fact that you, you know, occasionally cross the line."

"Well, I want to do what's right," I pointed out. "What's right involves a lot more than what I want, you know? Forcing someone to confess when they don't intend to…" I sighed. "It feels very much like something the Witches' Council would do."

"What do you mean?"

"There's a reason there's a constitutional right not to incriminate yourself. It's coerced. Even if she confesses, it's not entirely voluntary." I sighed again. "I'm not comfortable with it. And I'm even more uncomfortable that your eyes lit up like it was Christmas morning at the thought of it."

"Yeah, sorry," Emma said, shrugging. She didn't seem disturbed by the concept even as she apologized.

"You know, there's no Fifth Amendment in the magic world," Ayla pointed out.

"Millie Dallas is human."

Ayla snorted. "Millie Dallas used magic and ghosts to engineer all this. If she didn't abide by the rules of her world, she shouldn't get to take advantage of them now."

I turned in the front seat and "That's literally exactly how it works, Ayla. Even people that don't abide by the rules? Those rules have to be applied to their situation. The rules are for everyone."

"Maybe they shouldn't be," she murmured.

I frowned.

* * *

WHEN WE ARRIVED, an ambulance was there, but no one was moving as if someone's life depended on it. "Oh, please don't tell me she just up and shot her husband because she didn't want to wait for the divorce," Emma muttered, throwing the car in park. "That'd be twice the paperwork."

An ambulance crew was transporting a woman on a gurney, her hand dangling limply from the side and peeking out from beneath the white sheet pulled all the way over her face. I recognized the monstrous emerald ring on her finger.

We'd reached the end of Millie, if not the end of the case.

"What happened?" Emma asked the paramedic, flashing her badge.

"Husband said she climbed up on that big oak tree over there and fell out trying to stretch to get that small camera at the end of the branch," he said, pointing out the camera. "She landed on a pile of rocks. I'm guessing a broken neck."

"You guess?" Emma asked.

The paramedic and the cops exchanged glances and then shook their heads. "Lady, I don't have an MRI machine out here," the paramedic said with indignation. "From the bruises, my best guess is a broken neck. She's got a broken leg and ankle, probably a fractured pelvis, lots of cuts and abrasions—but that neck looks like what did it. She was already gone by the time we got here."

"You guys see anything?" Emma asked the officers.

"We were inside. Joe heard the husband and wife fighting." He raised an eyebrow. "Honestly, I didn't even know Mr. Dallas could raise his voice. He was always so quiet. Anyway, he said despite their issues, he always worried about Unity and had even gone so far as putting cameras on her house so he could prove to Millie that she wasn't doing half the things Millie accused her of." The officer pointed up. "Millie Dallas raced out of the house like her butt was on fire and scrambled up that tree before we could stop her."

"She wasn't very good at climbing trees, but boy, she was determined. Then she slipped, fell, and just stopped moving," the other officer said, pointing to the dead woman on the gurney. "Camera fell, too. It's an outdoor digital, so it survived. Just the lens is broken." He handed Emma the small surveillance camera.

"Okay, thanks," she said and turned away from them. Tapping buttons on the camera, she cursed a few times. "Damn it. How do you work this thing?"

"Here, give me that," I said, snatching it from her. "You don't even have gloves on." I turned it on, pressed some buttons, and a time-stamped image of the yard, and the oak flashed onto the screen. I backed it up to the early morning, around the time of the murder, and paused. It had night vision.

It also had a clear view through Unity's bedroom window.

There was Millie Dallas sitting on Unity's bed facing Unity, who was in bed but sitting up looking furious. The two women were talking animatedly.

Unity pointed toward the door.

Millie slammed her fist on the bed.

Suddenly, Millie stood, but the video blurred, almost like the camera was shaking. Maybe a squirrel running on the branch?

It cleared again.

Just in time for Millie Dallas to raise her gun at the old woman.

Unity leaped out of bed toward her, but she wasn't fast enough, and she collapsed to the ground. Dead.

"Wait. Where's the chest?" Emma asked, squinting. "I don't see it, do you?"

I paused the video for a few seconds before

fast-forwarding it at the slowest possible speed. Wynn Rogers walked in with the chest a half-hour later. He was startled (as if he didn't know what he would find) and dashed over to Unity Priestpoint to check for a pulse. We watched as he rolled the elderly woman over and began CPR, stopping periodically to shout frantically at Millie.

Millie pulled at him, seemingly intent on stopping the lifesaving measures.

Wynn shoved her back and then pulled out his cell phone.

She ripped it from his hand.

They appeared to argue.

After a few seconds, she shrugged and allowed Wynn to continue CPR.

Which he did for another ten minutes.

But it was no use.

"Well, maybe he tried to save her, but he didn't report it, and he didn't call 911, and he helped cover up the crime," Emma said with a sigh. "He's an accessory after the fact, and with this video, there's no argument. It's there in black and white."

"I didn't think he was telling the whole truth, but I didn't suspect this," I told Emma. "Somehow, his surprise and trying to save her makes everything they did a little worse." I sighed. "I feel like we didn't solve this. We just followed something around until it blew up."

Ayla poked me. "But if you hadn't followed it, Jason might be charged. Or Arthur. We turned over enough rocks that worms spilled out. That's something, you know."

"Yep, that's something," Emma agreed, shrugging. "Besides, Wynn is a sleazy lawyer that lies for a living. That we couldn't figure out where the lie was isn't a huge failure. In the end, all is right with the world. Ghosts freed, wrong people released, right people arrested." She looked up. "Well, as soon as we do it. Okay, I'm going to get this processed and then go arrest Wynn."

"And let Jason out?"

"Yep. And look at that! You didn't even have to violate the constitution to do it."

CHAPTER EIGHTEEN

I didn't know Cassandra had trendy restaurants, but apparently, the little psychic town did, indeed, have trendy restaurants —and Jason Bishop took me to one for dinner on Valentine's Day.

The tables were isolated from one another, flickering candles giving each two-seat table the appearance of being in its own self-contained world. We were at the back of the restaurant on the top of a multi-level deck overlooking the small town's Main Street. It flickered with pink lights.

Jason wore a suit and tie. He looked like he had just stepped out of a movie.

As opposed to, you know, jail.

There were plenty of men at the tables around us who were attractive in the same way, men who could walk out of a movie and look like they belonged there—and yet, something about Jason stood out from the crowd. He had a noble expression on his face that always made my heart skip a beat.

"Sorry, again, about the outfit," I told him, gesturing to my daily uniform that, depending on who you asked, looked like a scuba suit or an assassin's costume in a Jason Bourne stage show in Orlando. "I had no idea we were going to be dressed up. Even if I did know, I don't really have any other clothing, so..."

"It's fine," he said, leaning in. Jason's eyes met mine, and he gave a wide, friendly smile as if to reassure me his words were the truth. "This is our first date. Even if you'd shown up in sackcloth and ashes, I'd be grateful that we finally got to this point. No matter what you wore."

"I think sackcloth and ashes are a little much for a first date," I said with a grin. The waiter brought us some honey-glazed corn from the farm down the road, and as I took a bite, I also took a moment to really look at Jason. "I'm glad to see Archie didn't attack you at all while he was guarding you in the pokey."

Jason's laugh was rich and warm. "I think he was feeling too guilty about putting me there to even consider attacking," he said with a smile as he leaned back in his chair. "I think one of the guards had to get stitches."

"I know," I said, my face darkening. "And I'm sorry about that. It wasn't just him that got you stuck in there. If I hadn't tried to hide you from Emma—"

"She would have arrested me sooner," Jason said with a shrug. "And in front of my students. I'm grateful that didn't happen. It's a bit hard to reach kids after they've seen you dragged out of the classroom in handcuffs."

"Yeah, but—"

"None of it was your fault or your owl's. I was just in the wrong place at the wrong time." Jason held his hands up as I opened my mouth to apologize again. "Stop, Astra. I'm not going to let you apologize for someone else's mistake. You all worked it all out in the end."

The rest of dinner went by much the same way, with Jason making sure I understood it wasn't my fault every time I tried to apologize.

"So, Millie shot Unity to push Wynn's plan for her money into fruition. I understand that," Jason said as we sipped hot chocolate with a piece of dark chocolate on the side for me and a piece of white chocolate for him. "But I don't understand what Emma was telling my mother and the captain about all the magic stuff. What was that about?"

"I think Wynn just got fed up with Unity's treatment of her kids, and he had an interest in the occult, and Millie used that to push an agenda. She probably told him about her son, Jody." I paused and thought about it. "I mean, it's possible Wynn represented a client that told him about the paranormal world or maybe paid him with that ghost rock trap thing Ayla disappeared," I mused and then popped a piece of chocolate in my mouth. "Ooh, this is good. Anyway, the long and the short of it is they used magic manipulation to get money. Money that would have come to them when Unity died, but Millie didn't have the patience to wait."

"Yes!" A woman screeched three tables away. "Oh, my gosh, Terrance, yes! Of course, I will marry you!" I turned to find Terrance pushing up off his knee to wrap the excited woman in a passionate embrace while the rest of the patrons applauded.

"I always knew Terrance was a keeper," Jason

said, grinning at the couple hugging. "He was just too shy to ask her."

"You know them?"

He nodded. "They live here."

One waiter tapped a spoon against his glass, and the whole place fell silent. "I would like to make an announcement," he said in a deep voice. "It is with great pleasure to announce the charming couple I had the pleasure of serving tonight, Terrance and Hannah, have just gotten engaged. I know you'll all be happy to witness and celebrate this happy event with them." The room erupted into applause again as the two hugged once more.

"That is great news! Congratulations to the happy couple!" Jason called and raised his glass in a toast. Everyone else followed, and the outdoor deck turned into a bedlam of congratulations and celebration.

* * *

JASON TURNED BACK TOWARD ME, smiled, and held out his hand, palm up. "Give me your hand?"

I froze. "Why?" I asked sharply.

Probably too sharply.

The celebratory couples closest to us turned

and looked at me for a moment, irritated by the discordant note I had introduced into the love fest, but then resumed their laughter, joking, and drinking.

"Come on, just give me your hand," Jason said again, his eyes twinkling. "And I mean your hand, Astra. No glove."

Wary and watching for any movement that indicated Jason was about to drop to one knee, I took off my right glove and slid my hand into his. "Okay, now what?" I asked, images flashing in my mind like cards in a Rolodex. Within seconds, though, they faded away. "Huh. Weird."

"Close your eyes," Jason said and squeezed my hand. He curled his fingers gently into my palm. "Okay, now keep them closed, and just feel."

"Feel what?" I asked, but before he could answer, my hand tingled. It started at the top of my palm and ran up to my wrist and then down my arm. "What are you doing?" I said and tried to pull away, but he held firmly, keeping my hand pressed against his.

My eyes flew open. "What are you doing?"

Jason chuckled. "My mother taught me how to push everything out of my mind but a feeling. I know you can see images—"

"So, what, you were remembering the time

you stuck your finger in a light socket as a child?" I asked sarcastically.

"No, Astra." His eyes twinkled in the candlelight. "I was remembering how you make me feel when I see you."

Oh, jeez.

This was so not the right time for this conversation.

This was the first real date we'd ever had. We were in public. Other people would hear this— not to mention the hundreds of ghosts his mother probably had surrounding this table reporting back on our every word.

Yup. No way was I letting this go anywhere.

I froze, my mouth open and ready to deliver the sarcastic comment I was thinking, but all the words and thoughts drained from my mind. All I could do was stare at him. His face was so hopeful that I would like his "gift."

I swallowed. "Look, I'm sorry. I just—"

"No, don't apologize." He reached up and brushed a strand of hair from my face. "I'm the one who should apologize. I should have warned you. I know you can see images when I touch you, and that can be overwhelming," he said as the tingling expanded and ran up my arm.

"Not too overwhelming," I said through a gasp

as the tingling turned into a rush of warmth that spread all the way to my chest and beat against my heart.

"Are you okay?" he asked, his eyes filled with concern. "Do you want to take a walk?"

"I'm fine," I said, my voice sounding as if I were a hundred miles away, as the warmth turned into a radiating glow that filled me completely, blocking out everything but Jason.

"You look a little flushed."

"Yeah, I'm fine," I said through clenched teeth. "It's just—"

The warmth was intense, and I found myself stiffening and leaning forward. "Okay," I gasped as the room spun. "This...is...too much."

Jason released my hand, his expression concerned. "Did I hurt you?"

I shook my head and sucked in a deep breath. "No, but I think I need some air," I said as I pulled my hand back and put my glove back on. A second later, I realized how ridiculous that statement was. We were sitting outside in the moonlight.

The warmth that had filled me was gone, replaced now by a feeling of emptiness and a chill that ran through me. It wasn't like I felt cold. I wasn't trembling. In fact, I felt hot. My face was flushed, my eyes were smarting, and my hand was burning where he had touched me.

"Are you sure you're okay?" he asked, squinting and putting his hand under my chin, tipping my head up to look at him. Jason's features were composed, an air of easy confidence about him I sometimes envied.

I pulled away from his hand. "Jason, I'm fine."

The corners of his mouth quirked up into a smile. "Okay. I'm glad. You want to talk about it?"

"No."

He dropped it.

We finished our night with no more incidents or surprises, but just the memory of how I felt when he touched me was enough to rattle me more than I wanted to admit. Jason seemed slightly disappointed that I didn't want to elaborate on what had just happened, but he didn't allow it to spoil his mood.

By the time we pulled up in front of the house, things were almost back to normal between us. An easy casualness I enjoyed.

"I had a great time tonight." Jason looked at me. His gaze was suddenly intense. Then he leaned forward in the driver's seat, his position shifting to move closer. "Thanks for going out with me." He held my gaze as if he wanted something else, and then he moved ever so slightly forward again.

Oh, hell, no, I thought to myself. I knew exactly where this was going.

I opened the passenger door, hurrying to stop whatever subtle momentum Jason was building up. "I had fun, too. I've got an early day tomorrow, though, so I'm going to head in. Thanks for dinner."

He blinked. "I'll walk you to the—"

I slipped out of the car. "Goodnight!"

I slammed the door on his confused expression.

Look.

When I said that I was fine, I meant it.

But I wasn't ready for that. I didn't even know what it was that I felt from him.

Thankfully, by the time I got home, the feelings were gone.

And I wasn't ready to feel them again.

Not yet.

* * *

"THAT'S LOVE, YOU DOLT," Archie said as I changed for bed. I'd just given him a condensed version of the story, and he looked at me from his perch as if I needed my head examined. "You don't even realize it, do you? The guy is in love with you. Jeez, you're an idiot sometimes."

"Hey!" I warned the owl. I pulled back my bedding and settled into bed, pulling the blankets over me. "Manners."

Archie rolled his eyes. "Okay. Manners." He paused. "Art thou daft, my lady?"

I rolled my eyes. "No, but I wasn't ready for it. I don't like surprises. Surprises in the military? Never a good thing. Surprises are not good. I don't like them."

"I was a surprise."

"Yep." I didn't elaborate on whether that was good or bad.

"You know he's in love with you. Why are you just ignoring—"

"I probably just had too much to drink, and I was reacting to that. It's fine."

"Really?" he scoffed. "Tell that to someone else that doesn't know you're really good at not dealing with emotions and lying to yourself." Archie tilted his head as if confused by his own statement. "Well, I mean, you're good at lying to yourself. Like, really good."

I curled up, pulling the covers up to my chin. I didn't want to talk about this any more. "Hey.

Not trying to change the subject, but I really missed you while you were watching Jason at the jail. I know we had that whole 'we need to hang together' thing already with the gods, and you weren't abandoning me so much as making sure nothing happened to Jason, but…I missed you. A lot."

Archie hesitated but then launched himself off his perch and onto the nightstand. He cocked his head, staring at me. "You're trying to change the subject."

I sighed. "I still mean it."

"Thank you. Back at you." Archie bobbed his head. "You didn't have too much to drink. You're not stupid. You know when you're drunk."

"Whatever." I rolled onto my side. "I'm going to sleep now, so if you've got something to say, save it for tomorrow."

"Like you always do," he muttered as he hopped onto my pillow, his talons inches from my nose.

I sighed and sat up. I bent my legs under the blanket and put my arms around them, resting my chin on my knees. "Okay, let's go. Why are you harping on this so much?"

Archie blinked. His wing feathers slowly lifted and settled back down as he walked toward the edge of the bed and hopped back on the nightstand. "Your biggest weakness is that you lose focus on everything else when you're working. For years, you ignored your family because you didn't want to deal with them. Your life is better now that you're no longer doing that," he said, his voice low and serious. "You have no idea what the consequences will be if you decide to do that again with your personal life."

"I'm not ignoring Jason," I disagreed. "I went on the date."

Archie fluffed his feathers and settled them into place. "Oh, that's right. Your first date. How many months ago did you meet him? How long ago did he ask you? Are you really patting yourself on the back that you finally went on one single date with your proclaimed boyfriend? Seriously?"

"I don't know," I groaned, closing my eyes and putting my head back down. "You're right. He asked a while ago."

"And you refused him, right?"

"Well, you attacked him first, so that might have had a little to do with it," I said, my gaze still closed. I opened my eyes to find the bird staring at me accusingly. "Yeah, okay, I turned him down."

"And how long have you ignored him?" he asked. "This isn't just a question of putting him off because of your workload. This is ignoring the fact that he's interested in you. You're hiding from your feelings. That guy probably worked months to learn how to do what he did tonight. He gave you a *feeling*. His feelings for you. Do you know how romantic that is? He let you in." Archie leaned forward, his talons gripping the edge of the nightstand. "And you? You pulled away."

The bird was right.

"It's going to take some time, Archie."

"You know, I'm immortal. You're not," he snapped. "You mortals act like time grows on trees or breeds more like rabbits."

"I'm going to bed now," I said, sliding down and closing my eyes. "I'm tired."

"Are you going to do it?" he pressed. "Are you going to push him away again? Say you're not interested? Punish him for doing something nice for you?"

"No," I said, my voice muffled by the pillow.

"Pfft. You don't know yet." His voice was sharp, his meaning was clear. I felt him hop down off the nightstand. "I can hear it in your voice. What's stupid is you know exactly what you want," he added. "You just don't want to admit it to yourself."

"It's not that easy, Archie," I sighed and fluffed my pillow. "Let me try to get some sleep. We'll talk about it in the morning."

"I'm not going to forget you said that."

"I know you won't."

He crawled back onto his perch. "I'll be here when you want to talk about it."

And I knew he would.

* * *

THANK YOU FOR READING!

I hope you enjoyed Owl Melt with You. Please think about leaving a review! Astra, Archie and the whole Arden family continue their adventures in Book 7, Bring Your Beach Owl.

KEEP UP WITH LEANNE LEEDS

Thanks so much for reading! I hope you liked it! Want to keep up with me?

Visit leanneleeds.com to:

Find all my books...

Sign up for my newsletter...

Like me on Facebook...

Follow me on Twitter...

Follow me on Instagram...

Thanks again for reading!

Leanne Leeds

FIND A TYPO? LET US KNOW!

Typos happen. It's sad, but true.

Though we go over the manuscript multiple times, have editors, have beta readers, and advance readers, it's inevitable that determined typos and mistakes sometimes find their way into a published book.

Did you find one? If you did, think about reporting it on leanneleeds.com so we can get it corrected.

Made in the USA
Monee, IL
21 February 2022

91606445R00194